LA
EASY

Also by Dennis McKay

Novels
Fallow's Field (2007)
Once Upon Wisconsin (2009)
A Boy From Bethesda (2013)
The Shaman and the Stranger (2015)
The Accidental Philanderer (2015)
A Girl From Bethesda (2017)
Summer of Tess (2018)
Bethany Blue (2019)
In Search of Cloud People (2020)
Life and Times of Scruffy Lomax (2020)

Nonfiction
Terrapin Tales, with coauthor Scott McBrien (2016)

LA
EASY

Dennis McKay

LA EASY

iUniverse books may be ordered through booksellers or by contacting:

iUniverse
1663 Liberty Drive
Bloomington, IN 47403
www.iuniverse.com
844-349-9409

Book cover design: Megan Belford

ISBN: 978-1-6632-2919-9 (sc)
ISBN: 978-1-6632-2918-2 (e)

Library of Congress Control Number: 2021919470

Print information available on the last page.

iUniverse rev. date: 10/15/2021

CHAPTER 1

1995, Southern California

THEY TOLD THEMSELVES—ALTHOUGH NOT with complete conviction—that it had all the makings of one of their classic road trips, though they lacked one essential: their youth, the ultimate trump card. But, what the hey, they were currently in Monty's Bricklin and cruising up the Pacific Coast Highway, Los Angeles in the rearview mirror.

Passing through the Redwood Forest, Chad offered his hand toward the massive trees towering over them like watchful sentries. "The land of giants signals we are no longer under the pull of Tinseltown."

Monty accelerated out of the forest, the windy road hugging the undeveloped coastline. He flexed his fingers, his palms remaining on the steering wheel. "I feel *the pull* of the open road."

"Entering Big Sur does it every time." Chad looked to his right at the cliffs and the crashing surf pounding the shore.

"What's this," Monty asked, "our third road trip up the coast?"

"Fourth, but how many have we taken in all?"

"We've had some humdingers over the years."

"By my count this is our fifteenth," Chad said, "but our first in over five years."

"Yeah, should have listened to you," Monty replied in a hollow voice, albeit still maintaining the what-the-hell, boys-will-be-boys demeanor that seemed a part of his DNA.

"Gold digger found herself a pot of gold at the end of the rainbow thanks to her sugar daddy," Chad teased.

"Sugar daddy? Come on, Chad. It wasn't that bad."

"What are we, Monty," Chad said, his eyes grinning, "a couple of middle-aged guys in search of their vanishing youth?"

"For a couple of days anyway," Monty replied. "So, enough of the philosophical reality. Let us begin to live in our ephemeral cocoon of illusion."

"Ephemeral! Listen to you. Does that illusion include women?"

"Maybe, maybe not."

"Monty, back in the day you couldn't wait to get on the road in pursuit of young lovelies."

"Back in the day," Monty said, slowing down behind a tractor trailer hauling a double rack of new vehicles up an incline then entering the opposite lane, where he zipped past the hissing, whooshing semi and quickly moved back into the right lane, "we were a pair of heat-seeking missiles, weren't we? Me in need of a break from my realty firm, and you—"

"Getting rejected, yet again, for the lead in another low-budget film or made-for-TV movie."

"It was great therapy." Monty glanced at Chad with a look that said, *Agreed?*

Chad was tempted to ask if this trip would be great therapy, but he knew better. Monty—whose younger wife, whom he had been married to for five years, had recently left him for an even younger up-and-coming director she had met at an EST conference—had suggested that they take this road trip up the Pacific coast like the old days.

A road trip in Monty's sleek two-door, two-seat hatchback Bricklin sports car, which had been collecting dust in storage for years, was a first. They had always traveled in one of Monty's more expensive and reliable cars: Mercedes S-Class, Cadillac DeVille, and Porsche 911. Had the divorce affected Monty's decision-making? The Bricklin was notorious for unreliability.

Chad had told Monty before departure, "That fiberglass wannabe Corvette wasn't dependable brand new—only lasted two years! Now a tune-up is gonna make it all go good." But Chad pushed the issue no further, seeing that Monty needed this trip and, it appeared, needed to take it in his Bricklin.

They ate lunch on a cantilevered deck at the Nepenthe Restaurant in Big Sur, the rugged Santa Lucia Mountains, thick with oak and conifer trees, serving as the backdrop. Below them, a steep hillside of chaparral shrubs and stunted scrubby trees met a rocky shoreline, where land abruptly met the Pacific Ocean.

Chad chomped heartily into a club sandwich, his cheek puffing out. "Sooo, Mon … tay," he said, mayo oozing out the corner of his mouth, which he wiped with his napkin, "how is my buen amigo doing?"

Monty took a swallow of his beer and slanted a look out toward a one-man sloop skimming along past the break, tacking into the wind. "I have been in love twice," he said in a rare revelatory moment. "The second time I married her and never strayed—but she did, and it cost me half my net worth and my house in Malibu."

"Well, my friend," Chad said, holding a french fry up as though for emphasis, "Lord Tennyson said it best: 'Tis better to have loved and lost than never to have loved at all.'"

"All the years I've known you," Monty said in an even rarer moment of analysis, "I have never known you to be in love with a woman."

Chad shot a look at Monty—*Where the hell did that come from?* "Now, who is getting all philosophical?"

"Sorry, old chap," Monty said with a wave of his hand. "The divorce has brought out the melancholy analytical side of me." He crossed his hands in front of himself. "No more philosophy."

Chad smiled a casual okay, but Monty had inadvertently struck a vulnerable you're-all-alone-in-this-life chord that had recently surfaced in Chad's psyche.

Monty forked a portion of the house salad they were sharing onto a plate and stabbed his fork into a cherry tomato, then speared a slice of avocado and a few bite-size pieces of romaine lettuce. "Damn," he said, "that is a good salad." He narrowed his gaze at Chad as if to say, *Well, here we are. Let's enjoy ourselves.*

"Since," Chad said with a concurring nod, "we're taking this illusionary trip in remembrance of our youth." He looked directly at Monty to get his full attention. "Do you remember the first time we met? I was sleeping on the sofa of a friend of a friend."

Monty took a sip of his beer with a look of revisiting days gone by. "Yes indeed, the Oakwood Apartments, in dear old Sherman Oaks, back in"—he paused—"seventy-two?"

"Seventy-one," Chad said.

"That place had it all: tennis courts, fitness center, pool with barbecue patio, *and*—" Monty said in a tone indicating, *Your turn.*

"Outdoor basketball court with lights, where on my first day there"—the details hurtled through the staggered expanse of memory, appearing front and center in Chad's mind—"I hit the winning shot from the corner." He tapped his index finger to his temple, a mock question in his eyes. "Who did I hit that shot over?"

Monty winced. "Oh, I think you know very well." He leaned forward and rested his forearms on the table. "I gave you all you could handle, hotshot."

"Agreed. We were a good matchup, couple of young six-footers in shape."

"You were a newcomer to SoCal, a twenty-four-year-old—"

"I was twenty-five," Chad corrected. "You were twenty-four."

"Okay," Monty said, turning his attention to a table of college-aged women erupting in an outburst of uproarious laughter, which sounded vigorous, as if the whole group was recollecting a past escapade.

Monty caught the attention of one of the women, who threw him a look that said, *Hi there, handsome.*

Monty gathered himself as though trying to recall the subject at hand. Turning back to Chad, he answered, "Oh yeah, a young guy, twenty-five, who had recently quit his job with the federal government in Boulder, Colorado, and arrived at the Oakwood to pursue a career in acting."

"Tell you what sticks out in my mind about that day," Chad said, forking salad on his plate. "You picking up that bombshell actress at the swimming pool after b-ball."

Chad shoveled a forkful in his mouth, before chomping down. "Oh yeah, that is good." He pointed his fork at Monty and said, "You homed in on a dark-haired beauty with a body that had all the requirements: shapely legs, firm, plentiful breasts that were bulging out of her bloodred bikini top, and a pretty face with pouty nonchalance, that SoCal indifference."

"Yeah, she was sitting across the pool in a lounge chair, reading a paperback, with an occasional glance up as though expecting someone."

Monty squinted as the sun emerged from behind a billowy cloud, his shelf of hair glinting in the streaming light.

"After making eye contact, you presented your I'd-like-to-get-to-know-you smile." Chad grinned at the memory. "She then made a face as if to say, *Really?*"

Monty, who had the swagger and the chiseled golden-boy appearance of a matinee idol, returned his attention to the table of young women, again catching the attention of his admirer.

"You know you are old enough to be her father and then some," Chad said in a mild scolding tone.

"So I am, old chap," Monty replied. "Did I dive across the pool?"

"You did not come up until you reached the other side, where you popped out of the water directly in front of her."

A swarm of chirping swallows diverted Chad's attention as they soared and skimmed and maneuvered over the cliffs in search of insects.

"And?" Monty said, glancing at the group of young women, who were now departing.

"She looked at you as though seeing you for the first time and handed you her towel. That was the first I witnessed of many a seamless seduction by the Blond Bomber, Montague Sinclair."

"Another happy ending," Monty said. He smiled at his departing admirer, who returned the favor by pressing her three middle fingers to her lips and extending them toward him in a farewell kiss.

Back on the road, the Bricklin zoomed north up the coastal highway, its destination a four-star hotel on Monterey Bay, with a favorite tavern, where Chad savored pulling up a stool and ordering a cold one or two.

As much as Chad tried not to stew over it, he wondered if this journey would only highlight the fact that he and Monty were chasing memories from their youth. A youth that—at first so hedonistically wonderful—had over the years somehow conspired against Chad and led him to question his self-worth.

But on the other hand, why not spend a couple of days on the road, drinking a tad too much, while in search of, if not young lovelies, then an older version—and then worry about the rest of your life?

The engine strained a whining groan. Chad let out a sigh. "Like we didn't know this was gonna happen."

As the car began to lose speed, Chad lifted a finger toward a scenic overlook sign. "Half a mile to safety."

On an incline, the engine began to sputter, before the Bricklin belched a giant cloud and lurched forward.

"Son of a bee ... don't you dare die on me now!" Monty shouted as they neared the top, the car now barely moving.

When they were almost there, the engine let out a terrible groan and died, the car coming to a halt.

Monty put his foot on the brake and asked, "Chad, can you push me up and over, so we can coast down to the overlook?"

Chad pressed the button on the dash to open the passenger-side gull wing door. Nothing. "Thank God we don't have power windows," he said. He rolled down the window and twisted his way out headfirst. After checking his rear for oncoming cars and seeing none, he placed his hands on the car's rear and hollered, "Ease up on the brakes, Monty!"

The Bricklin was light and easy to push. Lickety-split it reached the top of the hill. Getting back into his seat was more difficult than exiting, but Chad got himself seated after squeezing himself in headfirst, with his back to the car.

They coasted down and off the road and onto a stretch of asphalt bordered by a waist-high stone wall that ran parallel to the ocean. The car came to a stop in front of the wall, providing a wide view of the Pacific Ocean stretching out in forever blue.

Chad gave his head a sighing shake. "Seriously, Monty, I say we hoist this fiberglass anachronism over the cliff."

"One good thing about this car," Monty said, lifting the receiver of the car phone situated between the seats, as though holding exhibit A, and called AAA. After a brief conversation with the dispatcher, he told Chad the tow truck was on the way.

"Will your door open?" Chad asked.

Monty pressed the driver's door button on the dash, and the gull wing door started to open haltingly, but stopped halfway up.

Once again, Chad squirmed his way out of his window headfirst.

Monty followed, sliding over into the passenger bucket seat and exiting the same way as Chad.

By this point, part of Chad wanted to head back home and forget this trip was ever considered, as he was beginning to realize it was time to grow up, but another part of him told him to see it through, if not for himself, then for Monty, who may well need time in the company of his best friend to sort things out. Having believed a road trip might be good medicine for Monty, Chad worried that regret may seep in and register, with stark clarity, that it was not this trip that was the illusion, but their lives.

While they waited for the tow truck, a two-tone VW van, lime green on the bottom half, white on the top, the two paint colors meeting and forming a *V* in the front between the headlights, pulled into the area of the overlook.

"Classic VW bus with wraparound windows no less," Monty commented as the van parked a couple of slots over. Painted on the driver's side was the peace symbol: a yellow circle with a red circumference and red diameter that was met by an inverted yellow *V.*

Two women emerged, one wearing a tie-dyed T-shirt and cutoff jean shorts, the other in a long sleeve T-shirt and slacks.

"Well, well," Monty said, as he eyed the woman in tie-dye. "What have we here?" She had sun-streaked blonde hair that she wore in pigtails, the kind of body that had drawn Monty's eye over the years, and a pretty, open face that had a free-spirited, go-my-own-way appeal.

"What kind of sports car is that?" the woman with pigtails inquired as she approached.

"Bricklin," Monty replied as he removed their luggage from the rear of the car. He looked in the direction of the VW. "What year is your van?"

"Nineteen sixty-eight. I bought it two years ago at an estate sale."

"With the peace sign?" Monty asked.

"Yes," she replied. "That more or less clinched it for me."

She took in Monty in a casual but flirting way, which he returned with his stance of affable congeniality—eyelids at half mast, well-formed head cocked appraisingly, the cleft chin jutted out just enough to notice. It was as though they had reached a mutual admiration, two beautiful creatures basking in each other's company.

The other woman, who had been staying back, came over. She wore thick-lensed wire-rimmed glasses and had dark brown hair that was tied in a ponytail. Her body was more linear and flat than that of her shapely friend. She looked like a bookworm, librarian type, definitely not Chad's type of woman. And, unlike the other woman, who was questioning Monty about the Bricklin, she had a quietness about her, an uncertainty. Chad could already see where this was going. Monty would end up with the bombshell and Chad with Miss Boring.

"That door," Pigtails said, as her gaze settled on the half-open driver's-side door, "brings to mind a bird with an injured wing."

"Gull wing doors," Monty said, "have a dual purpose."

"Gull wing doors?"

"Unfortunately, we are broken down or I would take you for a fly over the ocean."

"No?" the woman said, her gaping expression showing that she only half believed.

"Cara," the other woman said in a gentle scolding tone.

"I don't know, Maylee," Cara said with hands raised. "Anything seems possible nowadays."

The clanging rattle of chains and the whine of brakes announced the arrival of the tow truck.

While Monty talked with the driver, Chad made introductions to the women. "I am Chad Carson, and my friend is Monty Sinclair."

"I've seen you before," Cara said with a finger wag. "But not in a polo shirt and Bermuda shorts."

"I'm an actor," Chad replied with a shrug.

Cara jabbed a finger at Chad. "You were killed by Jason in *Friday the 13th*."

Their attention was diverted as Monty hollered over, "Chad, are we good here, or do we ride with the tow?"

Chad envisioned Monty and Cara hitting it off and shacking up, and him getting stuck with Maylee, Little Miss Quietude.

Cara glanced at Maylee. Seeing no reaction, she said, "We're heading north, if that helps."

Chad sighed an inward sigh and waved Monty over.

"Well now," Monty said, his attention fixed on Cara, "what fun would life be without a little of the unknown?" He lifted his chin toward the VW van. "We are now in the hands of Fahrvergnügen."

CHAPTER 2

"**W**HERE WERE YOU GUYS HEADING?**" Cara asked as the Bricklin, with its raised front end attached to the tow truck by a hook and chain, disappeared around a bend in the highway.

"Monterey." Monty gave Cara a knowing lift of the brow. "We have a cushy suite at a sweet little inn right on the water." The brow lifted higher as his close-the-deal smile emerged, a gorgeous, contagious smile that had sold many a house and seduced many a young lovely woman in his single days.

Cara lifted her brow. *Well now.* "We're heading that way." She slid a look at Maylee, whose face was a blank slate as though she had no opinion.

How seamlessly Monty and Cara had paired off, and by default, Chad and Maylee—LA easy. Or not so easy, because Chad hadn't a bit of interest in this plain Jane named Maylee, of all things, while Monty had scored a ten.

Maylee peeked at Chad; her lips crimped tight at the corners of her mouth, while her dark eyes glinted a hint of interest. "We do have room."

Chad sat on the floor in the seatless rear of the spacious van, back against the sliding door, facing Maylee. Monty was riding shotgun as Cara drove, explaining that they too were on a road trip. "Heading north with no particular itinerary other than camping at some point." She jerked her thumb toward the rear of the van, where two sleeping bags and a folded canvas tent were tucked in a corner. "Free room and board." She looked at Monty, her eyes brightening, holding his, as though to say, *Interested?*

Monty asked Cara what she did for a living, and she said she was an artist. "Van Gogh and Monet inspired me," she said with a glance over her shoulder to Chad, who nodded his approval.

Maylee asked Chad how he had gotten into acting.

Be nice to her, he told himself. "I had been in high school plays and summer stock during college but decided on taking a job with the federal government after graduation." The memory flooded back to him, when he had let himself down by not going for it. "But," he said with meaning, "after three years of sitting at a desk, I couldn't take it any longer and headed to LA. But without a Screen Actors Guild card, parts were impossible to get, so I had an assortment of grueling day labor jobs, and occasionally I played an extra in a movie or commercial, for which I earned less than I made as a laborer." He paused as he made a small but meaningful gesture. "I don't usually talk about myself—kind of boring stuff."

"Please"—Maylee turned her palm outward in front of her chest—"continue."

"Well, I got my break when I finagled an audition for a low-budget ski mask commercial, and the inventor, who was a dentist, told me"—Chad raised his hands and bent the middle and index fingers on each hand, indicating air quotes—"'I saw your headshot on your portfolio and said to the director, 'I like those teeth and that sunshine smile, and I want it.' Ta-da, SAG card."

"And that made a difference," Maylee said. "Your SAG card?"

"All the difference." Chad went on to explain that with his precious SAG card in hand, he worked his way up to roles on *Alias Smith and Jones, Kung Fu, M*A*S*H,* and mostly low-budget movies from horror films to romance.

"But I have never gotten a lead; instead, I'm typecast as the friend of the lead or former boyfriend of the heroine, or I have an incidental part with a few throwaway lines, and all with little character depth."

They exchanged looks; Chad was taking new stock of this woman before him, who removed her glasses and wiped the lenses with a tissue. Without her glasses, her appearance changed: her gaze was still shy but receptive; her cheekbones now looked higher, as if she had some Native

American blood; and her delicate nose complemented a well-formed chin. *Better,* Chad thought, *but still …*

"I sometimes ask myself, what if I had done it right after college?" Chad said.

"Life-altering decisions made at the beginning of adulthood," Maylee said in a tone that said, *Been there, done that.*

"Sounds like you crossed your own Rubicon."

"I guess we all do." A slightly bemused expression came over Maylee's face that seemed to transmit a knowing alertness. Chad surmised that beneath the exterior was a formidable mind. *Won't hurt to get to know her some.*

"Tell me about yourself, Maylee?"

"She is a damn fine writer," Cara interjected, with a glance in the rearview mirror.

Chad made a face at Maylee—*Aha!* "Does not surprise me." He offered an encouraging smile. "So, tell me about your writing."

"She doesn't like to," Cara answered, laughing. "You have to force it out of her."

"Cara," Maylee said in a tone of mild rebuke.

"How did you two meet?" Monty asked.

"Art festival in La Jolla," Cara said. "I was selling my art, and Maylee bought a painting of my impression of the Mojave Desert—she knew right away what it was."

"Of course she did," Chad said, as though he had just figured something out. "She sees things."

"Exactly," Cara said.

"Can we please stop talking about me as though I am not present?" Maylee asked.

Monty looked at Cara. "What say"—he glanced over his shoulder to Maylee—"that you ladies be our guests at the inn and that over a few cocktails we get to know each other?"

Chad had seen this coming, but now, though not drawn sexually to Maylee, he was okay with it, okay spending some time with her. The women in his life, and Monty's for that matter, were more along the lines of Cara—physically appealing, and if they happened to have a brain, then it wasn't held against them.

"How can we say no to Monterey?" Cara beamed a lovely smile on Monty, her teeth like deepwater gems. It seemed that the two of them had already reached an understanding.

Across from Chad, Maylee's attention shifted to him with a look of consideration, as though unsure where he stood and unsure where she stood with him, as though this was all new to her.

"We both love Monterey, Maylee," Cara said. "A historical place teeming with art and literature—right?"

"Well," Maylee said stretching out the word, as she stole a peek at Chad.

For Monty, Chad told himself. "I am in."

"For art and literature it is," Maylee said.

Yes, Chad was okay with it, but not rah-rah about it. He hadn't been rah-rah about a woman in a long, long time. Bombshells, bimbos, and young lovelies came and went. The last time, and the only other time, he had had anything resembling a relationship was back in the early seventies, when he had a weeklong romance with an actress on the set of *Gunsmoke,* in an episode titled "The Demise of Jim Grissom," that rocked his world.

They played a married couple whose marriage was threatened by a villainous outlaw who lusted for the wife of Chad's character. Chad and his coworker had hit it off right from the first day of shooting. And that evening they spent the night together.

Her name was Monica Healey, a comely woman with brunette hair and green eyes that gave her a flirtatious aura, one exuding beguiling intrigue. Each night after filming, Monica and Chad would return to his room and engaged in the most rapturous down and dirty sex that Chad had ever experienced. He was smitten.

The final day of shooting, Chad's character had already been killed off by the bad guy, so he waited for Monica back at the hotel, but she never showed. He discovered at the front desk that she had checked out. Chad was crushed. They had agreed to a farewell dinner the previous night, and he was going to ask if she wanted to see him again.

Over time, he realized that besides her physical desirability, Monica possessed a mysterious aura about her that drew him to her like nothing he had ever experienced. It was like an addiction.

Marriage would have been a disaster. Though if she had been willing, he would have done it. He had craved Monica, whom he later learned from a production staffer on a soap opera set that she had married a wealthy British tycoon and was living in London.

Since Monica's bruising rejection, Chad had avoided serious relationships. Under Monty's tutelage, the two men became a seal-the-deal pair of pickup artists—wham, bam, thank you, ma'am. But now, at nearly fifty years old, Chad found it had reached a new and revelatory stage—*been there, done that,* waking up in the morning in his bed with a stranger, or sneaking out of her bed in the middle of the night, never to be seen again.

With Maylee, there was no physical attraction, but it might not be so bad to get to know her, to talk with her, to understand her. Why exactly he felt that way, he didn't know. *Don't overthink it,* he told himself. *Go with the flow and see where it leads.*

CHAPTER 3

THE GULL COVE INN OVERLOOKED a granite outcrop. Off to the right of the inn was silky-smooth beach that arced inward, away from Monterey Bay. This was Chad and Monty's third stay at this charming hideaway of nooks and crannies with its stone facade with intricate wood trim and tall arches. It also offered a fine watering hole, the Stein & Beck Tavern.

The four of them followed a bellhop, who was pushing a luggage cart down a corridor, the walls displaying paintings and photos of Cannery Row and Monterey Bay, including an overhead photo of Monterey and a portrait of John Steinbeck.

They came to room number seven with "Stargazer's Suite" in a scrolled script below the number on the door, which they opened to enter a hallway equipped with a mini fridge, a wet bar, and a spacious closet. Farther in there was a pullout sofa and two comfy-looking armchairs, between which a nautical table, supported by wrought iron legs, occupied a good-sized sitting area, which was separated from the kitchenette by a two-stool oak bar.

There were two bedrooms off the hallway, each with en suite bathrooms, and a flagstone terrace off the sitting area.

The bellhop asked where the luggage should go.

"Just leave it there. We'll sort it out later," Monty said.

Maylee reacted to Monty's command with a frown, adjusting her glasses in a hurried movement.

Monty, who had an ability to take the temperature of the room, said in his "Don't worry, be happy" voice, "What do you think, Maylee?"

"Very nice," she replied in a detached voice of a particularly acute observer.

Chad, who had no interest in sharing a bed with her, wanted to tell her not to fret about getting stuck in a room with a man she hardly knew. He considered suggesting that he would take the couch, but he decided now was not the time to broach the topic.

Maylee opened the sliding door and stepped out onto the terrace, which was bordered on two sides by a trellised privacy fence covered in ivy. There was also a picket fence with a latched gate and with an arched trellis overhead, the fence facing an alleyway.

After Monty tipped the bellhop, the others followed Maylee out. In the middle of the terrace was a round wooden table with four Adirondack chairs.

"Sooo," Cara said, placing her hands on the back of an Adirondack, "what do the gentlemen have planned for this evening?"

Monty lifted his hand toward four empty stools at the corner of the bar. "We have an opening." The bar was only a quarter occupied, its being a Tuesday in April with tourist season not yet in full swing.

Chad considered the Stein & Beck, a classic throwback tavern with an upscale yet rustic appeal. The redwood bar had a dark reddish-brown hue; behind the bar were rows of liquor before a plateglass mirror adorned with an intricately scrolled frame. The dining area had a tongue and groove pine floor dotted with round tables and high-back stools, and with booths made of golden-brown oak running along two walls, three to a side. Oil lanterns hung from the finished crossbeam ceiling, giving the space a nautical feel.

"I love this place," Cara said, taking in the tavern with incremental turns of her head. On the pine-paneled walls, over each booth, were framed photos of John Steinbeck book covers: *East of Eden*, with a picture of James Dean forever young; *Of Mice and Men*, with George and Lenny walking beneath a skeletal tree and toward a faded blue sky; and of course *Grapes of Wrath*, with a line of old battered stake trucks on a dusty dirt road, the beds teeming with all the occupants' worldly possessions.

"That one of *East of Eden* is the billboard cover for the movie, which was inserted for later additions of the book," Chad said.

"Still, pretty cool-looking," Monty said. He tapped the bar as if to introduce a new order of business. "What are the ladies drinking?"

"I will have a Singapore sling," Cara said.

"Yes!" Monty said. "Me too." He shifted his attention to Maylee. "Cabernet for me."

Chad lifted his hand to the approaching bartender, a handsome young guy in his midtwenties dressed in a gingham shirt, with sleeves rolled up to the elbows, and a black bow tie. "Jason, isn't it?" Chad said.

"Yes." Jason raised a finger, then his eyes flickered with recognition. "Ah yes, Chad Carson, the world-renowned actor."

"A memory like a true-blue thespian, Jason," Chad said. "Let us have two Singapore slings and a cabernet, and I'll have a—"

"Bass Ale on tap," Jason cut in. "I may forget a name or a line but not what the customer drinks."

While Jason prepared the drinks, Maylee said to Chad, "Is he an actor too?"

"Yes, local theater mostly. I stayed here for a couple of days awhile back while on location, and he was trying to get his Screen Actors Guild card."

"Tough business," Monty said. "The stories I could tell about Chad's near misses."

Jason returned with the drinks. Chad inquired if he had gotten his SAG card.

"Nah," Jason replied as he placed Cara's drink in front of her. "I've gotten out." He served the remaining drinks, then said, "I found an investor for a bar I plan to open in town."

"Good for you," Chad said in as upbeat a voice as he could muster. "Acting in these parts is a weirdly brutal business."

"You made it, Chad," Cara said. She cradled her tall glass, pinkish red on the bottom half and clear on top, garnished with a slice of lemon and a maraschino cherry.

"I sort of made it."

Monty lifted his beer and said in a spirited voice, "A toast." The others raised their glasses. "To new beginnings and new friends," Monty said. His eyes caught Cara's: *We're good—real good.*

"Hear! Hear!" Monty added as all four glasses clinked and the evening began.

The women were sitting one on each side of the corner of the bar with Chad and Monty standing at their side, facing them.

"Tell us how you became an artist, Cara," Chad said. He was curious about Maylee's writing, but something told him to wait to ask her about it.

"Summer after eighth grade, I got interested in painting when I took an art class at camp and the teacher showed me some photos of Matisse's work—the bright, expressive language of color and drawing." Cara took a sip of her drink and licked her top lip. "By the end of the summer, I knew what I wanted to do with my life."

"I had no clue at that point in my life," Monty said, "other than looking forward to attending Mira Costa High."

"In Manhattan Beach?" Cara asked.

"Yup, it was like *American Graffiti* come to life."

"Beach boy. Playboy," Cara teased.

"All of the above," Chad said.

"Were you two high school friends?" Maylee asked.

"No," Chad replied. He took a swallow of his beer. "High school in Huntington, Long Island. Attended a small college in Maryland on a lacrosse scholarship."

"And you ended up an actor," Cara said. "Interesting."

Monty said, "Maylee, when did you know what you wanted to do with your life?"

"I am still working on it." She stared into her wine, then lifted the glass and took a careful swallow. A look passed over her face that made it known that she had nothing further to say on the subject.

Maylee and Cara were an odd pair, the beautiful outgoing artist and the shy introspective writer. They were an example of opposites attracting, though they each had cross interests in the arts. Both looked to be in their mid- to late thirties, and neither gave off the vibe of ever having been married.

After two rounds of drinks, the group of four moved to a booth.

While the women used the ladies' room, Monty said to Chad, "A favor, old chap."

"Let me guess," Chad said, "Mr. Sinclair would like the bedroom for the evening to have his way with the lovely Cara."

"You mind?"

"New subject," Chad said as the women approached. "Bogies at four o'clock."

"What are you two conspiring?" Cara slid in next to Monty, her light blue eyes fixing him with a knowing stare. "I believe, Maylee, that a plot has been hatched behind our backs."

"A plot, you say?" Maylee said in a voice partially engaged and partially remote, as she sat down next to Chad.

"In search of bliss—carnal bliss, no less." Cara jutted out her jaw and shot Monty a bug-eyed look. "And let me guess who the ringleader of this plot might be."

"Monty," Chad said with brow raised and a marveling nod. "You are in over your head, my friend—way over."

"And it sure feels fine," Monty replied.

The dinner was sumptuous. All four had creamy clam chowder that was loaded with clams; Cara had the lobster tails, which she described as "the best ever"; Maylee had the seafood stew, which she said was a winner; and Monty and Chad had what they always got here, Dungeness crab, which did not disappoint.

After the table was cleared, Monty wrapped his arm around Cara's shoulder, smiling his killer smile. "How about a drink back at our moonlit terrace, fair maiden?"

"I would like that," Cara replied.

Maylee's mouth twisted into a tight corner, as though unsure. Possibly it was her fear of getting stuck in a room alone with Chad, or possibly a fear that she was not pretty enough for him, or possibly a combination.

What the hell? Chad said to himself. "Maylee, would you join me for a walk?"

Maylee balled her fist beneath her chin, the gaze on her face the one of a person considering her options, before saying, "Okay."

Chad and Maylee meandered along a path above the bay, the sloops and larger sailboats aglow from the moon spilling silver light across the water.

"There's a view that Cara could paint," Chad said. They stood back from a cliff, the clap of the water lapping the shore and the ding of a ship's bell the only audible sounds.

"It is lovely." Maylee's tone was quiet, vulnerable.

"I am planning on sleeping on the couch tonight," Chad said.

Maylee let her eyebrows scrunch as she adjusted her glasses. "Cara is much more experienced and daring than I am."

Chad, caught off guard by her frank appraisal, lifted his hand to a flat rock a few feet from the cliff's edge. "Shall we sit?"

There was something forthright and honest about Maylee that, upon closer inspection, caused Chad to think that she was not so plain— more of a woman with potentially some hidden beauty as though her rather stoic countenance acted as camouflage, a mask. No, she didn't have the vivacious appeal or the desirable body of Cara, but ...

"What say we get to know each other," Chad said, "and we go from there?" He made a face: *What do you think?*

Maylee gave out a look—*I think I might like that.*

"Tell me about your writing."

Maylee studied Chad as though to determine his level of interest. "Well, I make my way as a travel writer for airline magazines and the like."

"Sounds glamourous."

"As I suspect with acting, it can be a grind."

"I am guessing there is more."

"I see I am not the only one who sees things." Maylee gave a lift of the brow—*Touché.*

"Tell me about yourself, Maylee."

Maylee folded her hands in her lap, palms up, and stared into them. "I want to write stories that people will care about and remember," she said with a lift in her voice.

"Did you always want to write?" It crossed Chad's mind that he was enjoying the company of this shy, somewhat intriguing woman.

"I was an avaricious reader as a child. *Charlotte's Web, Peter Pan*, all of Mark Twain, et cetera." She lifted her gaze out toward the twinkling grid of lights and the blue-black expanse of water before her. "And of course Alcott and Austen in high school."

"Laying the groundwork," Chad said. He was interested in what this woman had to say, though he did wonder what sex with her would be like, whether mechanical and stiff or wild and passionate as she let go of all her inhibitions, tearing off her mask to reveal a whole new side.

"In college I majored in English literature with a minor in journalism," Maylee said.

"I majored in business with a minor in English." Chad made a face—*How do you like that?*

Maylee added, "By middle of my junior year, an interest grew to write stories about people and their journeys through a lifetime or a period of that lifetime."

"Have you written any stories?"

"Yes. The first, a picaresque novel set in nineteenth-century England, I spent five years writing between assignments and whenever I had a spare moment."

"And?"

"It was not worthy, but I learned some things about the process of writing a novel."

"And?" Chad took her hand in his.

"My latest, *Desert Girl*, is about a dirt-poor girl raised by a single parent in Barstow that my literary agent has submitted to some publishing houses in New York."

"Were you raised in Barstow by a single parent—your mother?"

"You'd make a fine detective." She cleared her throat quietly and said, "Your turn."

"Like I mentioned, I grew up in Long Island—Huntington. I was the middle child between two sisters. My father, an ex-marine and World War II veteran who fought in the Pacific theater, worked at a foundry."

Chad glanced at Maylee to gauge her interest. This was all new territory for him, talking to a woman about his life, his upbringing, but it was upon him that at this point of his life it was time to open up, to look inward and maybe, just maybe, reevaluate.

Chad went on to tell how there was a distance to Richard Carson that neither he nor anyone else in the family could penetrate. He never spoke of the war or what he had gone through, but obviously it had left a scar.

Chad's mother, Delores, like the majority of the American women of her generation, was a homemaker. She was a competent and loving mother, but her husband's sullen quietness left a pall over the family. It was not a miserable childhood, but it was more like being raised by a single parent. Chad, a natural athlete, took to sports—basketball and lacrosse in high school. His father never attended a game or showed much interest in his son.

"A two-week hunting trip that my father took every year to Canada was like a cloud having been lifted over the Carson household." It came over Chad that he had never discussed this with anyone, not even Monty.

"During that time, my mother moved with a giddy-up in her step. And at dinnertime there were conversations about school, dances, or whatever came to mind. But as soon as my father returned, it was back to sullen time."

"Childhood can leave a scar," Maylee said. "*And* it can break you or make you stronger."

"Or," Chad said as a self-discovery formulated in his mind, "set you adrift, where you are cruising through life."

Maylee clasped his wrist, turning his hand over to examine it. "My mother used to get her palm read by a Gypsy woman, whom she became friendly with." She looked up at Chad, a wistful smile skipping across her face. "The woman more than once told her that her life would make a good country and western song." Maylee ran her finger along a line that coursed from the heel of Chad's hand up to between his forefinger and thumb.

Her finger gliding along his hand sent an unexpected wanting, not exactly sexual, through Chad. It was a touch that gave him more, much more, of a desire to be in her presence, to converse about things. Some sort of shift was taking place, but what it entailed was yet to be determined.

"Long lifeline," Maylee said. She took him in with a slant of appraisal. "Still cruising?"

"More like stalled in traffic." Chad secured his hand in hers. "But the breakdown of a car appears to be providing a detour to who knows where."

"An academic scholarship to Berkeley not only provided a detour but also saved me from a life of menial jobs." Maylee went on to say that her father had run off when she was seven and that she had not a clue if he was alive or dead. Her mother, a waitress at a diner, raised her only child as best she could. "But Mama did not have the wherewithal or education to get us out of the trailer park."

"Your brains and my brawn. How did you like the most liberal college in the United States?"

"It opened up a whole new world for me." Maylee pointed to the blue-black sky, aglow in starlight. "'Twinkle, twinkle, little star, how I wonder what you are!'"

"Barstow to Berkeley," Chad said. "Aha, I see the Big Dipper."

"And the Little Dipper," Maylee said, pointing. "Together they swing around the North Star like riders on a Ferris wheel."

"You should use that line in a story—beautiful."

"It's not my creation, but I think writers should share, not a complete idea for a story, but little tidbits here and there. We are all in it together."

Chad nodded, considering her words. "Actors do the same thing, mimicking the manner in which lines are delivered, the way they react to a line." He paused as the clap of water against the cliff drew his attention. "But," he said, raising his hand, "you have to be careful to ensure that these nuances fit you style, your demeanor, so that what you're trying to convey to the audience is received loud and clear."

Maylee studied Chad's face as though she had discovered a new layer of depth and, possibly, a new layer of comfort.

Only the intermittent slap of water on rock broke the stillness. Chad found himself at ease sitting next to this intelligent woman, who was growing on him, and with a name he had never heard before—Maylee. "I do not know your last name."

"Lee."

"Maylee Lee?"

"I was born and known as Mary Lee until I met Cara, who designated me as Maylee. She said it fit not only my inner self but also my exterior."

"You know what?" Chad said. "She was right. I could not imagine you as a Mary Lee."

CHAPTER 4

A SLIVER OF MORNING LIGHT PEEKING through the curtains to the patio's sliding door flickered on Chad's face, stirring him awake. He lifted the blanket off his chest and sat up on the sofa in the sitting area. The two bedroom doors were closed with nary a sound coming from either.

He went into the kitchen, made coffee, and took a cup out to the terrace. Last night ran through his mind. He and Maylee had talked for a good long while—two hours at least. She was unlike any woman he had ever been with. She had a reserve to her that was like an invisible shield, a stance, a countenance that said, *I am different. I am me. Tread lightly.*

In a dream last night, Chad and Maylee scurried through a dark forest, branches swooping down and striking them. Maylee fell and Chad picked her up, struggling against a strong wind, underbrush blowing all around. They came to a clearing. "I am good," Maylee said, and Chad let her down. At the end of the dream, they entered a field of wildflowers sunstruck with a rainbow of colors. Maylee, giving a hard look at the glorious meadow before her, warned, "I do not trust happiness."

Chad took a sip of his coffee and leaned back in his Adirondack chair, flushed with a distinct clarity of mind: what he had considered happiness was nothing more than external gratification that had left him with no foundation, no long-lasting relationship, his whole being unmoored and drifting along. He was damaged goods, a man who in his entire life had loved no woman.

Yes, there was the infatuation with Monica on the set of *Gunsmoke*, but that was not love. He had been with well over a hundred women, and never once had he said, "I love you." Never once had any of those women said, "I love you, Chad." And with that emptiness came a going-through-the-motions journey.

Prior to LA, there had been limited experience with women. In college, Chad had dated only two girls for the majority of his four years. Each relationship ended rather amicably; in both cases Chad and the young women realized marriage was not in their immediate plans. Chad had been fond of each of his former partners but was not in love with either. The same went for them.

Before graduating, Chad took the civil service exam and scored high in math. Offered a slew of positions at federal government accounting offices across the country, he, having never been west of the Mississippi, accepted a position as an auditor with a finance office for the Department of Commerce in Boulder, where he dated around some, but nothing serious.

Boulder, home to the University of Colorado, was like an idling station, where Chad continued much as he had done in college, playing club lacrosse and partying with his teammates. He enjoyed the big-time college atmosphere of Boulder with its breathtaking view of the Rockies and the bar scene at night.

By the time he notified his boss of his plans to resign, Chad had risen to a supervisory position. "You're the complete package, Chad," she had told him. "Not only a talent for the work, but also you have a way with people—a bright future lay ahead of you in government service."

But he found the work tedious, which only increased his desire to pursue an acting career. So, he took his government pension and the money he had saved and headed west, washing up at the Oakwood Apartments, where he and Monty became roommates within a week, whereupon everything changed—he changed. California had a vibe, a vitality, that jolted Chad.

Following Monty's lead altered Chad from *hello, nice to meet you—* to—*my place or yours?* As much fun as it was, especially in the beginning, when it was all so fresh and new, all the while, as Chad honed his skills in the seduction game, a hollow and remorseless attitude seeped in, taking more than it gave—much more.

Like Maylee's dedication to her writing—working five years on a failed manuscript—Chad needed to recommit to his career: hire a photographer for a new portfolio, with a great headshot; get in tip-top physical shape; and contact his agent about doing local theater, where a studio scout might rediscover an untapped talent. And while he was at it, he'd become a better man.

The rattling whoosh of the patio door sliding open startled Chad.

"All quiet on the set. Scene five, take thirty-two," Monty said through one of his shit-eating grins. He pulled back a chair, placed his cup of coffee on the table, and slipped into his seat. He was barefoot, wearing jean shorts and a white undershirt, his hair disheveled, his face flushed as though he had just finished a morning jog.

But it wasn't jogging that had put a glow in Monty's cheeks. "Another notch on the bedpost there, Studly?"

Monty took a long, slow sip of his coffee. "Ah, good java," he said, giving a nod of confirmation. He placed his cup back on the table and leaned back, a bemused grin working the corners of his mouth. "Cara would like us to visit the Monterey Museum of Art today."

"Ooh, is the real estate magnate now into art?"

"Cara informed me that the museum collects, preserves, and interprets the art of California from the nineteenth century to the present time. How could anyone possibly refuse?"

"Refuse?" Chad said. "Cara being smoking hot would not have anything to do with this newfound interest?"

"You are so jaded, my thespian pal. Oh yeah," Monty said with a wince and an emphatic shake of the head, "I called the garage where the Bricklin was taken. The engine is shot."

"Well, you have told me over the years that part of the adventure was the risk of the unknown," Chad said. "What is Mr. Sinclair's plan B?"

"Now, why do I think you already know the answer?" Monty said with a conspiratorial twinkle in his eyes. His expression abruptly changed. "You okay with Maylee and all this?"

"Yeah, she's starting to grow on me."

Cara and Maylee came out onto the patio. Both women appeared showered and fresh, wearing polo shirts, shorts, and sandals. And it registered for Chad that neither was wearing a bit of makeup. There was a wholesomeness about both women, the blonde beauty and the reticent brunette.

"Are you in, Chad?" Cara asked.

Maylee stood at Chad's side, her hand on his shoulder.

"For the Monterey Museum of Art or joining you ladies on the road?" Chad said.

"Go big or go home, pilgrim," Monty piped in, using a dead-on John Wayne voice.

"Thank you, Duke," Chad said with a crooked salute off his brow. He turned to Maylee. "A *detour*?"

"Beats stalled in traffic," she replied.

The Monterey Museum of Art, a two-story adobe structure with a red-tiled scalloped roof and a clean and neat exterior, was situated in Old Monterey, the downtown district.

Inside, Monty stepped up to pay the admission fee after a wave of the hand to Maylee, who had offered to pay. "I buy, and you and Cara guide me and Sir Laurence Olivier."

"There is a photography exhibit I want to show you," Cara said, with a westward-ho toss of her hand over her shoulder to indicate the corridor.

Chad had heard of Ansel Adams, a famous landscape photographer known for his black-and-white images of the American West, but was unfamiliar with his work.

At each photograph hanging on the wall, Cara pointed out the intricacies. "Note the sharp focus and full tonal range," she said in front of a photograph of Yosemite Valley. In the foreground was a rocky creek bed; in the background, a threating sky looming over an arc of pine trees. Chad found the pure majesty and depth of the images breathtaking.

Cara pointed to a work titled *Lodgepole Pines*. "This is one of my favorites."

Along the banks of a fork in a river, tall pines dominated the scene, cracks of sunlight and blots of darkness between the thickets of trees. And on the water, the sandy-brown riverbank contrasted mostly in light.

Maylee extended a hand toward the photograph, her expression that of a person in deep concentration, as though on the cusp of discovery. Her mouth opened in a small circle. Nodding as if she had found her answer, she said: "Sitting on the banks of the Merced River, / Absorbed in the darkness and light, / I imagine my future in peaceful flight. / But if I soared high above the shadow and glow, / Will I still maintain my eternal flow? / Only one way to know, but do go slow, / For the unknown is a mystery, so caws the crow."

"Where did that come from?" Monty asked.

"She just conjured it up out of thin air," Cara said.

Chad settled his gaze on Maylee. *Who is this woman?*

She met Chad's eyes and said, "When my muse calls, I try to answer."

"Let us take Maylee and her muse to the Matisse gallery," Cara said as she headed for the exit, extending a pointed finger, indicating, *This way.*

The Matisse exhibit had a variety of prints, some in bright colors, others more muted, but all were "a distortion of reality," as Cara so succinctly put it.

They were standing in front of *Les toits de Collioure*, a painting of a French village with hills in the background.

"The bright colors appear more an emphasis than the drawing," Chad said.

"Hey now," Cara said. "You are on the money."

"I was just going to mention that," Monty said.

Cara squinted at Monty. *Doubtful.* She turned her attention back to the artwork. "Bright, expressive colors is one of the keys of neomodernism and, in my mind, the seeking of simplicity from the complexity of a changing world."

"To me," Chad said, lifting his hand toward the work of art, "you could extract complexity out of the simplicity of this drawing through interpretation."

Maylee said, "You are full of surprises, Monsieur Carson."

Leaving the museum, Maylee suggested lunch at a restaurant with what she said was a spectacular view.

The Surf House's outdoor cedar deck sat high above the Pacific, near to a thicket of cypress and pine trees sweeping down to meet the sea. The four were seated at a table positioned along the two-foot-high stone wall that ran along the deck's perimeter.

The crash of the surf pounding the shore was faintly heard, but the waves were not seen as the forest blocked the view of the shoreline.

"Green landscape meets deep blue sea, backdropped by a cloud-streaked sky," Chad said with one hand extended. "Spectacular indeed."

"Listen to you, Monsieur Connoisseur," Monty teased.

The waitress came over and handed out menus. Chad and Monty ordered beers, and the women asked for iced tea.

"May Maylee and I order for the table?" Cara inquired, lifting her menu.

Chad and Monty made dot-dash eye contact. "Yes," they replied in unison.

"Steamed mussels," Cara said with a lift of her brow toward Maylee, who nodded her approval.

Maylee ran her finger down the menu and stopped. "Avocado toast."

"And," Cara said, closing her menu, "garden salads all around."

"Perfect," Monty said.

And perfect it was. The steamed mussels were moist and oh so sweet; the crispy toast and mashed avocado was mouthwatering; and the garden salad was fresh with a succulent honey vinaigrette.

After the waitress cleared the empty plates and bowls, Monty said to the table, "Well, what do the Fahrvergnügen sisters have planned next on our schedule?" He said the word *schedule* with a British twist, putting emphasis on the *ch* sound.

"Maylee and I thought for our"—Cara swept her hand out to her side like a game show host—"driving enjoyment that tomorrow we should head north to parts unknown." She extended an open palm toward Monty, followed by the other to Chad. "Care to join us, gentlemen?"

"We are at your mercy, fair maiden," Monty said, "for our Fahrvergnügen is no more."

Chad looked at Maylee to reconfirm that she was okay with this. She said, "Don't you just hate it when you lose your Fahrvergnügen?"

The ride back to the inn was a quiet affair, Monty trading looks of admiration with Cara behind the wheel, Maylee writing in a notebook for what Chad surmised was some future story—about who knew what.

This was the first road trip Monty and Chad had taken that others were involved in, and the others in this case were women no less—astute and perceptive women. In the past they had had a specific destination— Baja, Palm Springs, Vegas, or any other resort that tickled their fancy— and off they went.

It all now seemed rather mindless ventures, drinking to excess and picking up and seducing women, whom they wined and dined. They were a pair of confident guys entering town in one of the expensive cars Monty had owned over the years. At first, Chad had been a tad embarrassed riding in such luxury, but soon enough his embarrassment faded.

They were like a pair of hunters in pursuit of game. While Monty possessed the laissez-faire air of a strikingly handsome dude, Chad was more the nice-looking boy next door with broad shoulders, a well-proportioned build, and a full head of sandy-brown hair that helped frame a balanced face anchored by a sturdy chin.

"You have your grandfather Carson's determined Scottish chin and, of course, those gray-blue eyes that shall catch many a girl's fancy," Chad's father's sister—Aunt Becca—had told him on a visit when Chad was in high school. But Chad was too shy back then to catch any girl's fancy, until he asked a girl to the senior prom.

It wasn't until he moved to the Oakwood Apartments and met Monty that Chad became a different version of himself.

"Pretend you are auditioning for a part," Monty would tell Chad when approaching young lovelies at a bar. They'd go to the windswept beach bars in Manhattan Beach loaded with flight attendants and beach bunnies; to upscale joints in Malibu, where there was a selection of older women, some divorced and wealthy and eager to have their way with young studs like Chad and Monty; and to Westwood, with a selection of fine bars with both a variety of college girls trying to break into acting and a number of professional women.

The entire LA scene back in the early seventies was an awakening for Chad. Such fun it was, especially after he got his SAG card and began getting parts. A young woman might approach him in a bar and ask if she knew him from somewhere.

Monty would lean across the bar and say with confident charm, "He's Chad Carson, actor extraordinaire, an up-and-comer soon to be seen in theaters across the gloo—oobe."

"Yes," the young woman would say with a finger wag, "you were on *Marcus Welby*."

At first, Chad had basked in the recognition and the many doorways it opened to a night of guilt-free sex. But as the years wore on, it slowly but oh so surely began to lose its luster. Truth be told, the sex with attractive women had never gotten old, but the lead-up and aftermath had definitely lost its shine.

And to Chad's surprise, it was Monty who changed the paradigm, telling Chad, "I've met the woman I want to spend the rest of my life with."

Sandy, the former Miss Arizona, was both fifteen years younger than Monty and a voluptuous gold digger. Whenever Chad was in her company, it was as though she were putting on an act, smiling and laughing on cue, but beneath that gorgeous exterior, he sensed there was a predator on the loose in search of a big-game husband. He couldn't believe that Monty couldn't see this also.

So, Chad broached the subject with Monty, who, for the first time in their friendship, got seriously angry with Chad. "Don't ever again tell me who I should and shouldn't marry—got it?"

Yes, Chad did get it, not mentioning a prenuptial agreement or that Monty may well be going through a midlife crisis to which getting married was his answer.

For the first couple of years of Monty's marriage, Chad saw little of his friend, just a few times a year at a party or an occasional afternoon get-together. Happy as a clam with married life, Monty told Chad at a deli in Beverly Hills, "We are talking about having a child."

But by Monty's third year of the marriage, Chad began seeing more of his friend, as Monty's married bliss had begun to fade, with Sandy spending more and more time at Beverly Hills Tennis Club, which she had insisted Monty join. Lunch or a beer after work was no longer spent with Monty talking about having a child or how happy he was with his wife; now it was about how his marriage had entered unknown waters. "If she isn't at the club playing tennis or getting lessons from Alfredo—the Italian stallion," Monty said through a withering sigh, "she is over there doing I don't know what."

Soon after, Chad spotted Sandy walking down Rodeo Drive holding hands with a handsome young man with wavy dark hair who had the look of a Euro jet-setter—Alfredo no doubt. The pair gave the impression of a young couple in love.

It was as though Sandy wanted to be seen. Chad had considered telling Monty about it, but he held back, Monty's having mentioned that he wasn't sure if she was still faithful since they hadn't had sex in months. Chad reasoned that telling his good friend what he already knew would only increase Monty's misery.

By year five of the marriage, Sandy had hired a savage divorce attorney. Before Monty knew what had hit him, he was no longer married—and with a big loss in the pocketbook. "At least it wasn't the Italian stallion," Monty told Chad one night over many beers at Chad's house. "She not only has played her husband," Monty said through a *stupid me* face, "but also decided on door number three, an up-and-coming producer who's even younger than she."

And now Monty was single again, but this time it was different. He and Chad were older, damn near fifty—though a youthful fifty—and the two women they had met were different. Maylee and Cara had depth of character and intellect. Where it was all leading, Chad had nary a clue, but like with a good movie, he could not wait to see how it all ended.

Back at the inn, Monty suggested they go to the swimming pool. "Let's catch some rays and decide on what we want to do this evening before you ladies hijack us to parts unknown."

"That will work—catching rays, that is," Cara said coyly. "The hijacking part, I will leave with you and your twisted imagination."

So, they headed back to their suite and changed clothes, the guys in bathing trunks, Cara in an aqua-blue bikini that highlighted her curvy body and radiant tan. She and Monty were a golden couple, physically a perfect match.

Maylee wore a dark-blue standard women's bathing suit, her lean body lacking the curves and bulges that usually garnered Chad's attention, but it was not her physical appearance that drew him. Rather, it was her nimble and perceptive mind capable of spinning out a thought-provoking poem off the top of her head.

At the L-shaped pool, all four sat in chaise lounge chairs, facing the water. It was a gorgeous day, crystal-blue sky, warm yet comfortable, and only one other group in attendance, two couples in their seventies playing cards.

As Cara and Maylee applied sunscreen on themselves, Monty said, "There are grills and picnic tables on the inn's private beach. All we need are some burgers, and franks, paper plates and we're good to go."

"Maylee and I don't eat pork or red meat." Cara motioned for Monty to sit up and swivel around so his back would face her.

"Well," Monty said, as Cara began to rub sunscreen on his shoulders, "how about shrimp on the barbie?"

"With roasted zucchini, butternut squash, and red onion," Maylee said, handing her tube of sunscreen to Chad.

"I bet old Chad wouldn't mind if you applied that lotion on him," Monty said.

Chad's immediate impulse was to throw a hard look at his friend, but he caught himself. "Healthy veggies on the side sounds great," he said. He displayed the lotion in his open hand, glancing at Maylee.

Maylee took the lotion and motioned to Chad to turn. "I bet you two were quite the pair of Lotharios back in your heyday."

"Hey, now," Monty said with an expression of mock hurt, "we are still under the illusion—"

"That you are still twenty-five?" Cara cut in.

"More like thirty-five," Chad said, enjoying the smooth, firm touch of Maylee's hands and fingers circling his back.

"Illusion, confusion," Maylee said in a singsong voice, "drives the male ego to the edge as he ponders *his* future without one *ounce* of hedge." She leaned forward, her small yet firm breasts grazing Chad's back, and reached around to apply the sunscreen to his chest. Her body against his, and her words, struck like a one-two combination of carnal and mental acuity. She was getting to him.

"Question, Miss Maylee," Monty said, as he nodded a thank-you to Cara, who had finished her task. "Do you incorporate your poetry into your writing?"

Maylee tapped Chad on the shoulders—*All done*—and said to Monty, sitting sideways on his chaise, "Not consciously, but sometimes when I have reviewed my work for the day, I am surprised by the rhythm and flow of the words."

"Wouldn't you say that poetry and fiction accomplishes the same thing?" Chad said. He sat back in his chair. Overhead, a lone cloud, puffy, floated across the sky. "That the goal is to tell a story with a moral or some type of resolution at the end providing a new perspective or reinforcement of ideas?"

"Yes," she replied.

"Observation," Monty said with an air of joviality. "If my Lothario sidekick and I are not careful, you two artful and intelligent women will be the ruination of a beautiful thing."

"Or your resurrection," Cara said.

CHAPTER 5

WHILE MONTY AND CARA WENT out shopping for the cookout, Chad and Maylee returned to the suite. They were sitting on the terrace, each with a glass of cabernet. Usually in this type of situation, Chad would have been trying to finagle a way to get her in bed. But with Maylee, he did not want to hurt her, have his way with her, and after this trip never see her again, as he had done with other women so many times in the past. But knowing himself well enough to know that old habits were hard to break, he figured a conflict may emerge between his old carousing ways and his new conscience.

Though he could tell Maylee was attracted to him, Chad was not sure she was ready to go all the way, which could change everything. Had a devastating relationship in the past contributed to her cautious nature, or was this just the way she was? Either way, he did want to be with her to talk with her or to enjoy the silent pleasure of being in each other's company.

"What are you thinking?" Maylee asked.

"To be perfectly honest," Chad said, "how different you are."

"From whom you usually go out with?" Maylee took a sip of her wine. She lifted her brow as though to say, *Am I right?*

Chad eased back in his Adirondack. "It's nice to find someone to talk with, to get to know and discover what's ..." He threw his hand in front of himself. "And see what's under the hood."

"Careful," Maylee said, "I just may steal that line from you."

They both started to speak at the same time, and Chad said, "Please, go ahead."

"I was going to say," Maylee said, "when I first saw you and Monty back at the overlook." She folded her hands on the table, a smile flickering at the corners of her mouth. "My first impression was that you were a couple of good-time Charlies in your exotic Bricklin."

She brought her elbows on the table, hands folded under chin. "But since we're being honest, I liked you from the first, a nice-looking man who I sensed"—she fluttered her hand in the air as if in search of the right words—"from the way he held himself, had a transition taking place."

"Oh my," Chad said, "I'm in the presence of a witchy woman."

They looked at each other for a moment, and in that moment, there came another of those shifts, those internal quickenings.

"In a way, Monty and I have lived charmed lives, or so it seemed."

He glanced at Maylee, her eyes saying, *Please continue.*

"First off," Chad said, "we both avoided Vietnam."

"Terrible, unnecessary war."

"After graduating in '68, I was classified I-Y from a knee injury from college athletic days that has long since healed." Chad placed his hand on a barely visible two-inch scar on his left knee. "And Monty, who's a year younger and graduated a year later, was eligible for the draft lottery and received a high number. And then," Chad said, his past flooding back, "living the swinging singles life in Southern Cal back in the day."

"I sense a *but* coming."

"Maybe," Chad said carefully, "Too much of a good thing isn't all that good for you."

"Sometimes ... people change." Maylee placed her hand atop Chad's, scanning his face as though trying to ascertain if her statement were true in his case.

Chad put his face in hers, his lips on hers, their mouths opening, their tongues intertwined.

"Would you," Chad said in a careful voice, "consider sharing my bed tonight?" He lifted his hand as though taking an oath. "Not for good-time Charlie reasons, but just to be with you."

Maylee paused for a moment and gave out a look. *Possibly.*

"Fair enough," Chad said with a lift in his voice. "The gentleman's proposal is under consideration by the fair maiden Maylee."

Cara and Maylee prepped the shrimp and vegetables in the kitchen—olive oil and diced garlic on the shrimp, and salt and pepper and oil on the vegetable medley, which they prepped in aluminum foil trays that they would place on the grill for cooking.

As they exited via the gate to the patio, Monty raised a bottle of Chablis in one hand and a bottle of cabernet in the other. "Good wine," he said, his face breaking into a delighted smile. He lifted his chin to the plastic bag of shrimp that Chad was holding. "And good food." His voice was picking up steam, as though he were onstage introducing the lead act. "And last but definitely not least, good women."

"Monty," Cara said in a teasing voice, "you are so full of it."

Monty closed the gate with a gentle kick, the hasp clicking into the latch. "My dear Cara, it takes all kinds to make the world go round."

On a perfect little crescent of beach, Chad emptied half the contents of a small bag of charcoal into the grill and asked for a match.

"Uh-oh," Cara said. "Not a smoker among the four of us."

"Fear not, I got these at the front desk." Maylee pulled a pack of matches from the back pocket of her shorts.

After Chad got the fire going, they settled on a flat rock facing the water, which was lapping gently against the shore. Behind them, the sun was heading toward the western horizon, the sky over the water streaked purple and orange. There were a few motorboats puttering across the bay and also sailboats of varying sizes, their sails catching the wind.

Monty poured cabernet into two plastic wineglasses and served them to Maylee and Chad, then a glass of Chablis each for himself and Cara. There was a bit of a chill in the air. The women were wearing hoodies. Chad was in a flannel shirt; Monty, in a long-sleeved T-shirt and V-neck sweater.

Chad slipped his hand into Maylee's, her warmth sending a charge through him. It might prove difficult to keep his promise about only lying next to her.

"How 'bout that," Monty said, pointing toward the water, "a wooden-hull schooner with three jib sails."

"It's lovely," Cara said.

The sailboat was gliding across the bay, its white sails bending with the breeze, propelling it forward.

"You don't see many with wooden hulls anymore—mahogany, no less," Monty said with a trace of remembrance in his voice, his gaze settling on the boat cutting across the water.

"Did you sail?" Cara asked.

"Did he ever," Chad said. "He used to like nothing better than competing in a regatta."

"Really?" Cara said. "You mean golden boy had other interests beside his puerile desires?"

Chad picked up a stone lying in the sand and flung it. It landed short of the break. "Mast man. Wasn't that your duty, golden boy?"

"Like the Lone Ranger?" Cara said through a laugh.

"No," Monty said evenly. "*Mast*, not *mask*. I worked with the foredeck to hoist the gybe-drop spinnaker and help hoist and drop the genoa sail."

"Listen to you, sailor boy," Cara said.

"Sailor … boy," Maylee said in her melodic, rhythmic voice, indicating a poem incoming: "Said ships ahoy, how far must I sail? / And when the sky turned dark and the boats were stowed away, / Sailor boy lost his desire to maintain the fire / That burned only on the open sea. / But that burning desire did not expire / As he transferred it ashore in the pursuit of girl named Lorelei. / When she left, he took new steps / In the pursuit of hot flesh, from sea to shining sea."

Silence fell over the group as though a great truth had just been unveiled.

Monty blurted a what-the-hell laugh. "Maylee, you cut right to the bone."

"Sometimes my—"

Monty cut in, "No, Maylee, your insightful poem was on the money." He raised his wineglass, took a sip, swallowed, and exhaled through his teeth. "But her name was Cary Ann, not Lorelei."

Another quiet spell fell over the group before Monty said, "I might as well get the whole truth out." He looked at Cara, his bravado replaced by open-eyed credulity. "The second time a woman left me cut way deeper." He paused. "My younger ex-wife, Sandy, recently divorced me for an even younger man."

The last time Chad had seen this side of his friend was when Monty had bared his soul over many beers after Sandy had dumped him. But this time, instead of a regretful, woe-is-me confessional, there was an honest, naked truth, not only to his words but also in his look, which said, *This is me.*

Cara placed her hand on Monty's cheek. As their eyes met, she leaned into him, kissing him very gently on the lips. She leaned back, her compassionate eyes on his. "That took courage."

Cara then stood. "Maylee," she said, shifting her attention to the grill. "Shall we cook?"

As Cara and Maylee tended the grill, Chad and Monty sat and sipped on their wine.

"How are you doing, Mr. Bricklin?" Chad asked in a soft voice.

"Better, with still a ways to go," Monty replied. He glanced over at the grill, where he saw Cara and Maylee standing side by side, tending to the shrimp and vegetables with plastic forks. "We have something in those two over there, my friend, yes indeed."

Chad was struck by this new side of his good friend, a revelatory side. At the same time, there was an incremental transformation building within. Where it would lead, only time would tell.

"Shrimp on the barbie, gentlemen," Cara said, setting a plate of seared shrimp on a nearby picnic table, the bodies of the succulent crustaceans, still in the shells, streaked yellow and pink, the tails a charred orange.

Maylee placed the plate of vegetables down, stealing a conciliatory glance at Monty, who said in his affable voice, "Smells and looks incredible."

And incredible it was. The shrimp was tangy and succulent. The richly colored medley of the dark-orange squash and golden-yellow zucchini with green skin pockmarked from the heat, along with the caramelized red onions, was "delish," as Monty said. When they were finished, there was nothing left but shrimp shells.

"Idea," Monty said as he folded his arms on the table and leaned forward, hunching his shoulders so that his chin sat against his neck.

"Do tell, Sir Monty," Chad said.

"A beach campfire?"

"I like that," Maylee said. She lifted her glass of cabernet to Monty. "Grand idea."

"While you guys dig a pit," Cara said, "Maylee and I will collect dry seaweed and driftwood."

"Now we're talking," Monty said, eyeing a level area off the beach of sandy dirt and a smattering of reedy grass. "Right there looks like a good spot." He leaned his shoulder into Chad's. "Would not my dashing thespian compadre agree?"

"Si, senor, es buena idea."

"El hombre speaks Spanish?" Maylee asked in a half-kidding, half-impressed tone.

"Enough to get him in trouble," Monty replied.

Chad finished his wine and wiped his bottom lip with his forefinger. "I spent six weeks in Yelapa, Mexico, picking up some of the lingo while filming an adventure film, where I had the lead, that never got released. Kept my streak intact." He shrugged, "Que sera, sera, amigos." He shrugged again, a little too casually, and stood. "Let us get a fire under way."

By the time the fire had taken, night had settled over the bay, with a fat yellow moon floating in a starlit sky. The four sat on the ground around the crackling blaze, which launched red-hot embers up into the air before dying out.

They sat reflectively as though digesting the events of the last two days. Chad's hip was against Maylee's, his bare leg grazing hers. This woman who upon first meeting he had considered a plain Jane was now taking hold of him, her presence growing inside him.

When the fire grew weak, they headed back to the inn. Chad and Maylee, as though on autopilot, slipped into her bedroom.

"Well, here we are," Maylee said. She took in the neatly made king-sized bed, the thick pillows double stacked, the linen duvet folded precisely at the foot. Pulling the covers back on one side of the bed, she slipped in.

They lay in bed, Maylee with her back to Chad, nestled into him, both in shorts and T-shirts. He breathed in her warm scent of sweet wine and fresh air tinged by the smoke from the campfire, her hair whisking his face, her breathing coming in a soft rhythm similar to her poetry.

"How are we?" Maylee whispered in a sleepy voice.

Chad wrapped his arm around her waist and nuzzled the side of his face into her neck. "Good," he lied.

Maylee rolled over, squinting, without her glasses on. She leaned forward, planting a kiss on his cheek.

This woman whom at first he'd had no desire to be with had gotten under his skin, and along with this came a desire to make love to her like she had never experienced before. But he sensed that it would not go over well. He concluded that the purpose of her kiss was to say good night.

Maylee pulled back and said, "Thank you for understanding."

In the past Chad would have not surrendered so easily, but this time, with this woman, it was different. And, he hoped, he was different. He turned on his back and pulled the covers up under his chin, saying, "See you in the morning."

CHAPTER 6

Aᴏᴛᴇʀ ʙʀᴇᴀᴋꜰᴀsᴛ ᴀᴛ ᴛʜᴇ ɪɴɴ, they packed up and stowed their bags in the spacious rear of the VW van.

Monty dangled the car keys. "Madam Monet has allowed me the honor of chauffeuring you fine folks for the day."

"Very gracious of you, madam," Chad said.

"Chad, you sit up front with Monty," Cara said with a lift of her hand. "Maylee and I will navigate from the rear."

Inside the car, Monty said to Cara, who was sitting in a cushioned seat on the floor, her legs extended, "Where exactly are we heading?"

Cara looked across the van. "Maylee, what do you think?"

"Yosemite."

"Yosemite it is," Cara said.

"Which way?" Monty asked as he pulled away from the inn.

"Go east, young man. Go east," Maylee said.

"Thank you, Miss Greeley," Monty said, tilting his head toward Maylee, who was sitting behind Chad.

"This puttering bus must be a big comedown from your Bricklin," Cara said.

"Not a problem for Mr. Bricklin to switch to Mr. Fahrvergnügen," Chad said. "Especially when there is a beautiful woman involved."

"To thy own self be true," Maylee said. "Would Mr. Fahrvergnügen not agree?"

"Agreed," Monty said, pointing to an overhead sign indicating the CA 1 toward Salinas. "Take that?"

"Yes," Maylee said.

"Well now, I am asking meself," Chad said with an Irish lilt, "how Sir Monty feels to no longer be driving in the fast lane." He jerked his head toward Monty, a lopsided, cartoonish grin plastered across his face, which brought an uproar of laughter from Cara and a tee-hee from Maylee.

"If nothing else, I am adaptable," Monty said. Just then an aqua-blue Stingray Corvette convertible, with a young guy driving and a pretty blonde woman in the passenger's seat, her abundant hair blowing in the wind, roared past.

An accident outside Salinas brought traffic to a snail's pace.

"Idea," Cara said, as she scooched up between Chad and Monty, a hand on each of the front seats.

"Why do I think we are about to undertake a new flight pattern?" Chad said to Cara.

"Let's detour to San Jose," Cara said. "I know a great place for lunch atop Mount Hamilton."

"Let's hike up from the base," Maylee said, coming up next to Cara, behind Chad. "Does that not sound grand, Chad?" She placed her hand on his shoulder.

"Monty, old chap," Chad said with a thespian flair, his voice tinged with a British aristocracy, "you did not tell me that one of the conditions of this hijacking was trekking up a mountain for sustenance."

"Now, now, Sir Laurence," Monty said, "part of this hijacking adventure is the unknown, the curveball with that special twist."

"Now that we have that settled." Cara pointed to an exit sign—US 101 North, toward San Jose—and said in a singsong voice, "'Do you know the way to San Jose?'"

"'I've been away so long,'" Chad trilled, "'I may go wrong and lose my way.'"

"That's why providence brought Cara and me onto the scene," Maylee said. She grabbed the rear of Chad's seat, her head over his shoulder. "Angels sent down to guide the wayward back into the fold."

"Sounds like the making of a story," Monty said.

"Or a poem," Maylee said.

"Go for it," Monty said.

She recited the poem, as follows:

> In one's journey in this life,
> There are obstacles along the way,
> But if one is observant,
> As an old wise man might say,
> The paradigm shifts
> In such an altering way
> That what was once considered ordinary
> Becomes the sublime.
> And in the end,
> A new door opens
> And *he* is no longer blind.

Maylee directed Monty to the entrance of a state park at the base of Mount Hamilton. He paid the entrance fee and parked in a gravel lot. There was a ranger station, where they used the restrooms and changed into footwear more suitable for hiking, the women in ankle-high hiking boots, the guys in running shoes.

Maylee led them to the trailhead, where a wooden sign stated it was an eight-mile loop up and back down the mountain.

"How did you two know about this?" Chad asked as they began the climb on a dirt trail, into a pine forest. They were walking four abreast, the women in the middle.

"Maylee wrote a story for an airline about San Jose." Cara picked up a stick leaning against a tree. "Ah," she said, holding it up for inspection, "perfect walking stick."

"Well," Monty said, "that would make Maylee our resident expert on San Jose."

"The article was mostly on the history of the town," Maylee said. "The Conquest of California, the Mexican–American War of 1848, the Treaty of Guadalupe Hidalgo, which doubled the territory of the United States—that sort of thing, up to the invasion of high tech."

"Did you come here and research the story?" Chad asked as they came to a bend in the trail, with thickets of trees and underbrush as far as the eye could see.

"One week, all expenses paid," she replied as she motioned high up. "There," she whispered, "a red-tailed hawk."

Perched on a branch was the bird of prey, scanning its domain below.

"Full-grown adult," Maylee said. "Female, I'd say, by its large size."

Chad looked at Maylee, his eyes smiling at this bit of knowledge.

Maylee raised her hand to stop, her eyes lifted toward the hawk. "I wrote an article on bird watchers a few years back—it's beautiful," she whispered.

The bird cocked its head in their direction, its dark brown eyes taking in the interlopers with a look of intense appraisal. It flapped its dark and white checkered wings, and flew off.

"Wow," Monty said. "That was something."

As they started walking, Chad said, "A lesson in ornithology and history in one neat package."

"It's amazing," Monty said, "the intricate history in each town in our country, the world actually—so much to learn, so little time."

"Vigorous exercise brings out the philosophical side in Sir Sinclair," Chad said.

A chipmunk darted across the path in front of the walkers and into a burrow at the base of a tree.

"Best get into that hole, little fella," Monty said, "before the big, bad hawk has you for supper."

"More philosophy?" Cara teased.

"No," Monty replied, "just sound advice."

Two hours of trekking up the mountain brought them to an inclined clearing of sagebrush and wild grasses.

"Grandview Restaurant," Maylee said with a lift of her gaze up the trail, "is right around the bend up ahead."

"Hallelujah," Monty said. "I was about—"

Cara cut in, "To suggest we go back down and up again before lunch?" She lifted her walking stick and held it in front of herself as she high-kicked forward like a majorette with an oompah-pah flair.

Monty stopped and exhaled. "I thought I was in decent shape, but you girls put me and Chad to shame."

"Speak for yourself, Monsieur Bricklin," Chad said, as he kept pace with Maylee and Cara, who resumed a normal pace.

"Voilà," Cara said. They stood before a set of timber steps that led to the restaurant, a masonry structure painted white with tall storefront windows and a wraparound deck.

"That deck looks perfect," Cara said, taking the first step.

They were seated at a table along the deck's perimeter.

"What do you think, Chad?" Maylee asked. She lowered her gaze down the mountain, which was speckled with trees and brown patches of scrubby plants. "Is the view worth the hike?"

Chad took a gander at the valley, its patches of dry golden vegetation in contrast to a ribbon of misty hills in the distance meeting a glowing pale blue sky. "Absolutely," he said.

Monty said, "I think I deserve a cold beer or two after that twisting steep walkabout."

"Remember, my friend," Chad said, "you have to get yourself down the mountain."

Monty lifted his finger to the approaching waitress. "My dear, I will have the tallest, coldest beer you have."

"Incorrigible," Chad said. He then ordered an iced tea, as did the women.

The meal was delicious all around. Monty had a juicy, oozy cheeseburger and crisp fries; Cara, a salmon salad; Maylee, a Greek salad; and Chad, a club sandwich and tangy house salad.

Maylee beat Monty to the check and insisted on paying. "You can leave a generous tip, Monty."

"Before we depart down this twister of a mountain trail"—Monty lifted his mug and took the final swallow of his twenty-four-ounce stein of beer, offering a satisfied smacking sound—"might I inquire as to what plans the ladies have for our evening accommodations?"

"We are saving that … old chap," Cara said, mimicking Chad's accent when saying "old chap" with a perfect upper-crust English lilt. She laughed, tipped her head to the side toward Monty, and smiled a furtive smile. "After you get yourself down the mountain."

"Aha," Chad said to Maylee, "more intrigue for our weary souls."

"Intrigue has a plethora of meanings." Maylee lifted her face to Chad.

Chad looked closely into Maylee's eyes and noticed the brown orbs, but also something he hadn't noticed before, tiny flecks of amber like stardust in a dusky sky.

Maylee continued, "Secret plans ... fascination ... a mysterious quality ... or all of the above."

The trek down the mountain was uneventful—and much less stressful than the journey up—though by the time they arrived at the trailhead, all four were fatigued. Monty, with beads of perspiration dotting his forehead, had a vacant, pooped-out look. For Cara and Maylee, their eyes were reflectively drawn in as though they were thankful to have experienced such a day. Chad was experiencing a general achiness but also had a sense of well-being, not only from the invigorating exercise, but also from the sense of camaraderie with his best friend and Cara, and of course Maylee. She was growing on him in a subtle way as though her essence were sinking into his bones.

Cara leaned her walking stick against a tree. "Who is up for a campout?" She arched an eyebrow toward Monty: *What do you say?*

Monty's mouth pooched open. *Huh?*

"I suspect," Chad said, fighting a grin, "that Sir Bricklin was hoping for a four-star resort with a hot tub and well-stocked bar."

"You forgot a restaurant with a Michelin star or two," Monty said. He raised his hands in surrender. "But I shall serve the wants of the fair maidens of Verona." He bowed and swept his hands out to the sides. "Sir Bricklin at your service, Maid Cara."

"And you, the other sir?" Maylee said to Chad.

"I would not miss it for the world," he replied.

Maylee directed Cara to an outdoor supply store, where Chad and Monty purchased a tent and two sleeping bags. Then they went shopping at a supermarket. Last but certainly not least, they went to a liquor store.

"Okay," Monty said as they crossed the street from the liquor store, "tell me that wherever you are hijacking us to has a shower."

"Men," Cara said as she opened the sliding door to the van and placed a box containing four bottles of wine into the rear. She looked over her shoulder at Monty, giving him a quick once-over. "Don't want to get all earthy with me, huh?" she said with mirth in her voice.

"Monty," Maylee said, hooking her forefinger onto her baby finger, "there are bathrooms." She paused. "With toilets," she added, her forefinger moving down to her ring finger. "And"—she feigned trying to remember—"*and*," she said, her forefinger moving down again, "showers!"

"Yay," Monty said as he slid a twelve-pack of beer between the front seats. He and Chad got in the car.

Monty stretched himself out across the length of the rear, his head on the seat cushion. "Permission to nap until arrival at destination, madam?"

"Be my guest," Cara said from the driver's seat.

How smoothly Monty had slipped back into being a laid-back guy after baring his soul to the group earlier in regard to his divorce. But that was a consistently admirable part of Monty: whether it was a problem in business or his personal life, he worked his way through and got on with things.

Cara had assisted in that transition by not batting an eye when Monty revealed his failed marriage, her only concern being his well-being. They gave off the impression of being the perfect pair. It wasn't just their beauty; it was also the manner in which each reacted to the other.

Chad had never seen Monty so comfortable in the company of a woman, including his ex-wife, but could Monty's interest in Cara wane, his having so recently been burned by Sandy?

It was late afternoon by the time the van arrived at the campgrounds, located in a state park on the other side of Mount Hamilton.

"I believe if we had trekked down the opposite side of our way up, we would had arrived right here," Chad said to the front seat. Across from him, Monty lay sprawled out, dead to the world.

They were waiting in line to the entrance station behind two cars ahead of them. "Yes," Cara replied, "we are on the other side of the mountain."

"Oh ... yes, my muse is calling," Maylee said. "The other side of the mountain, / Where true love may be, / In the journey of a girl called

Maylee." She looked over her shoulder at Chad, taking him in, in full measure, as though she knew his darkest secrets.

"What now, young prince, as the mating dance unfolds? / What truth hath thee that have yet be told?" She raised an eyebrow with an expression of calm intensity. "Look no further than into thy heart, for there lies / The answer whether to stay or depart."

Chad reached up and put his hand on Maylee's shoulder. He held it there until they had entered the campground, and then he woke Monty.

CHAPTER 7

WHILE MAYLEE AND CARA UNFOLDED their tent, staked the corners with a ball-peen hammer, connected the tent poles, and assembled the frame, Chad and Monty were still reading the directions.

"Very impressive, ladies," Chad said as he opened a packet of pegs.

"Would you gentlemen like our help?" Maylee said a little too pleasingly.

"We got it," Chad said. He and Monty unfolded the tent and spread it out.

They were in campsite 22, an open, level space. Nearby was a lake, where the ranger had informed them there was a picnic table and grill. It was right near their spot.

"Well then," Cara said, "we will prepare a campfire while you Boy Scouts erect Maylee and Chad's guest suite."

Chad peeked at Maylee, who caught his look and returned a keen little smile. *All righty now. Things are looking up.*

By the time the men had finished setting up the tent, the sun had sunk below the tree line. Twilight tiptoed across the skyline. The women had the campfire crackling. All four sat around on the ground with drinks in hand.

"A toast," Monty said, lifting his beer bottle, "to fate and the flawed design of the Bricklin."

"Ipso facto," Cara said as all four clinked wineglasses and beer bottles.

"Exactly," Chad said. He lifted his gaze out toward the moon, which was rising over the tree line, the first glimmers of moonlight reflecting off the lake. He raised a hand as though to add gravity to his words. "The resultant effect is—"

"Yet to be determined," Maylee said.

"Yes indeed," Monty said. "So let us enjoy this time in our lives and see where it leads." He took a long swallow of his beer and wiped his mouth with the back of his hand. "Agreed?"

"Agreed," the others said in unison.

After two rounds of drinks, they moved down to the picnic table by the lake.

"A movable feast," Monty said, placing a bag packed with their dinner on the table.

"A feast is an abundant meal accompanied by entertainment," Cara said as she removed paper plates from the bag. "What do you have planned?"

"How about," Chad said, opening a plastic container of vinegar coleslaw, "Monty and I reenact a scene from a movie?"

"Yes!" Cara said. "Can Maylee and I pick the movie?"

"If we both are familiar with it," Chad replied.

"Let us discuss it over this sumptuous cold meal," Maylee said as she opened a container of baked beans.

"Beans, coleslaw, potato salad, and canned salmon," Monty gushed, "followed by an Academy Award–winning performance." He lifted his beer, arm extended straight out to Chad, who clinked his bottle with his.

Chad found the simple meal utterly wonderful. The food tasted yummy. The conversation was clicking as they discussed what film they should choose for the performance.

Casablanca, The Way We Were, and *Five Easy Pieces* were all suggested and discussed, with no unanimous choice.

"I've got it," Cara said, "*Butch Cassidy and the Sundance Kid.*"

"What scene?" Monty asked.

"That's easy," Chad replied. "The scene on the cliff—'Who are those guys?'"

"I will be Sundance," Monty said.

"You look like him," Cara said with a look around the table: *Doesn't he?*

"Well, Butch," Maylee said, "are you up for this?"

"I know that scene inside and out," Chad said as he scraped the last forkful of beans off his plate.

After Chad took Monty aside to go over the scene, they returned to the table. Dusk was settling over the land.

"Since Monty is not an actor by trade," Chad warned, "though he has been putting on an act his entire life." He paused for effect, eyes on Monty as if to ask, *Is that not so?* "We will sort of wing it, if you will."

Chad opened his hands to the women with an overly dramatic expression on his face. "We will perform sitting up against that little hill, under the light of the silvery moon." He pointed in the direction of a three-foot bank near the lake.

As they walked over to base of the hill, Chad set up the scene explaining that Butch and Sundance had been doggedly pursued by a super posse led by legendary lawman Joe Lefors. "We are cornered on a cliff high above a fast-running stream."

Chad and Monty took their positions against the bank, facing the water, the women sitting in front of them, legs crossed. A slant of moonlight reflected off the water like a mini spotlight on the performers.

CHAD AS BUTCH. They're going for position, all right.

MONTY AS SUNDANCE. Better get ready.

Chad stole a peek at Maylee, who appeared absorbed in the performance, with wide-eyed wonder at what she was seeing. It came over Chad that he wanted to give the performance of his life for her and only her.

BUTCH. "Kid, the next time I say let's go someplace like Bolivia, let's go someplace like Bolivia."

SUNDANCE. Right, next time.

BUTCH. Ready?

SUNDANCE, *projecting a look of utter disgust.* Not really.

Chad was so into this scene that he was in unknown territory.

BUTCH, *smiling as an idea comes to him.* We'll jump.

SUNDANCE, *with a look of incredulity.* Like hell we will.

BUTCH. No. It'll be okay. They will never follow us.

SUNDANCE. How do you know?

It crossed Chad's mind that at this very moment in time he was Butch Cassidy. He was on that cliff with only one rational answer to an irrational situation.

BUTCH. Would you jump that if you didn't have to?

SUNDANCE, *shielding the sun with a hand.* Just one clear shot.

BUTCH. They'll kill us.

SUNDANCE, *nodding as though considering.* Maybe.

BUTCH. All right, I'll jump first.

SUNDANCE. No.

BUTCH. What's the matter?

SUNDANCE. I can't swim!

A whirlwind formed in the pit of Chad's stomach as he unleashed an avalanche of laughter so pure and real that it stunned him.

BUTCH, *roaring with laughter.* Why, you crazy? The fall will probably kill you.

(*Both stand and pantomime jumping off the cliff.*)

BUTCH. Uh-oh …

SUNDANCE. Shiiiit!

The women stand and applaud. "That was great," they shout.

"Monty," Cara said, "you *were* Sundance. Awesome!"

"Who knew?" he said with hands flung out wide, pantomiming great surprise.

Chad caught Maylee's eye, and in it he saw appreciation and something else that he could not put a name to but that had settled into the core of his being.

Back at the campsite, the fire had died down. It was now smoldering and glowing as an occasional cinder flickered up and away before disappearing into the night.

Monty collected driftwood along the shore and restoked the fire.

With adult beverages in hand, all four sat around the fire as the events of the day brought on a period of reflection.

A sense of well-being came over Chad, something that he had not experienced in a long, long time, if ever. The performance with Monty had rekindled his passion for acting, a passion he had not experienced since his days doing summer stock. What an adventure that had been, setting up the set on outdoor stages or inside tents, all the actors pitching in.

The troupe traveled across Pennsylvania and Ohio performing *Death of a Salesman*, for which Chad had won the role of Biff, Willy Loman's talented yet wayward son. It was a big coup for twenty-one-year-old Chad to have been awarded the part.

At the end of the last performance, the director took Chad aside and told him, "The sky is the limit for you, Chad. You have all the necessary skills and the right look to go far onstage or on the big screen."

But after Chad had graduated college and scored high on the civil service exam, his mother—who had struggled during the Great Depression—convinced him to forgo acting in favor of choosing "the safety and security of the government." But after three boring years sitting behind a desk, he decided to take the plunge and headed to California, where he met Monty and, in the process, reinvented himself.

Though he had attained a level of success that many of his fellow actors would consider successful, Chad recognized now that he had let himself down, let his talent down. Part of it, he told himself, was bad luck; part of it, he knew, was a lack of motivation that had stealthily set in.

But now, that impromptu skit he had just done with Monty in front of Maylee and Cara had set something off in Chad, encouraging him to seek roles where he could display his talent in full. Whether it be a small part or a lead, he wanted to give all that he had to the character.

Maylee was sitting close to Chad, her arm around his waist, filling him with a wanting desire for a woman whom a few days ago he'd had zero interest in.

"Butch," Maylee whispered in his ear, "I don't have to jump." She took his chin in her hand. "But I am going to anyway."

Chad leaned his face into her neck, lightly kissing his way up to her earlobe, which he puckered between his lips. "Shall we?" he said.

Chad leaned back and stood, offering his hand, which Maylee took. She rose. He led her into the tent.

CHAPTER 8

MOONLIGHT SLIPPED THROUGH THE FRONT flap, casting their shadows on the walls of the tent. Chad and Maylee were atop the two sleeping bags lying side by side, facing each other.

"I have not been … with a lot of men," Maylee said in a hesitant, confessional voice. She leaned her head back from Chad, her elbow cocked on ground, her chin planted in the palm of her hand. "First time, I'd rather not talk about. The second was a one-night stand in college. Never saw him again—lesson learned."

Maylee breathed in and out, her shoulders rising and falling. "Number three was a six-month affair with a fellow journalist that ended when I discovered he was married."

In the muted light, Chad could not see her face clearly, but he sensed she was experiencing a cathartic moment, as though transmitted in mental pulses from her brain to his.

He placed his hand on Maylee's shoulder, which hunched before relaxing, and brought her in close.

"And number four," she said with a lift in her voice, "is a handsome actor who, to my surprise, has taken a liking to me."

"And, for the record, number four has never been married and plans on seeing you again." Chad leaned into her, his lips finding hers. He kissed her with passionate restraint. She positioned her arm under his, her fingers on his back, pulling him in tight and close, bringing a clamorous desire. He felt a need not only to have her but also to be with her.

Without prompting, they began the process of unclothing each other, until they lay in each other's arms naked. Chad felt the arousing sensation of Maylee's taut body entwined with his.

The lovemaking was tender yet forceful, each with avarice, lustful hunger. Maylee grunted with thrusting pleasure as Chad increased his stroke, until they climaxed, bringing a self-satisfied exhale from both.

Chad started to speak, then thought better of it. He remembered a line from a forgotten movie he had performed in: "In the silence of the night, there is much you can learn."

They lay on their backs, the *chk-chk* rasps of crickets breaking the silence of the night.

Maylee reached for Chad's hand, her nimble fingers sliding between his, her grip firm and oh so welcoming. This woman was what had been missing in his life. She appreciated who he was and who he could become. He had gauged all that in the manner in which she took him in with those eyes, which seemed to know him completely, her face showing some heightened sensitivity and understanding.

Where they were headed, he did not want to overthink. Enjoy each moment and let it come as it may.

Chad and Maylee awoke early as the first streaks of sunlight tottered over the horizon, penetrating the morning mist over the lake.

There wasn't a peep coming from Cara and Monty's tent. Maylee had gotten a map of the park when they had checked in. Looking at it now, she ran her finger along a trail that circled the lake.

"Four miles around the lake," she said with a lift of her chin toward the water. "What do you say, Chad?"

"Sure," he said. "And after, a swim in the lake?"

"Sounds like a plan," Maylee said with an uptick in her voice.

"Now that we have that settled," Chad said, "let us walk and talk."

As they headed toward the trail, Chad lifted his finger as an idea came to him. "And if the lady so endeavors, a poem would be welcome."

The trail meandered along a rise above the lake on the outskirts of the park. The forest floor was covered in a thick blanket of pine needles with a smattering of leaves.

They walked along at a good pace as the last remnants of morning mist dissipated off the lake, the sun rising up into a cloudless blue sky. Chad had said walk and talk, but Maylee's expression had forwarded itself to someplace faraway—possibly her creative mind contemplating verse? Or was she comfortable in the silence?

The splash of a fish breaking the surface of the lake brought them to a halt.

"From the corner of my eye I saw it leap," Maylee said.

"I missed it," Chad said. "Could you tell what it was?"

"Smallmouth bass," Maylee said as they began to walk again. "I wrote an article on sport fishing for a travel magazine and learned my fish."

"What's it like going to a place and learning about the subject matter and then writing a story?"

Maylee pursed her lips in a silent *hmm*, before giving a "Here I go" look at Chad. "Gather information from the appointed ones. / Listen and learn about the subject at hand / 'Til the fog has lifted." She motioned toward the now clear lake. "And one is gifted a cohesive account, / 'Til the mission complete, / But the time you spent, you cannot repeat."

Maylee paused, considering. "For time is a thief tiptoeing away / With more than it brings. / But just once I would like a moment / That held eternity in the essence of *things*." She had said the word *things* with a final twist as though putting a spin on a ball.

"Bravo," Chad said as they arrived at the other side of the lake directly across from their campsite. He spotted the figure of a man, wearing a red sweatshirt, at the water's edge.

Chad cupped his hands around his mouth and hollered across the water. "Olly olly oxen free!"

Across the lake, Monty raised his hand in greeting and then cupped both hands to his mouth. "Eee-yaw-kee!"

There was an eager note in Monty's voice, its sound floating across the water, where it hung suspended in a faint echo before fading into the trees surrounding the water.

"Come out, come out, wherever you are," Maylee hollered across the water, her voice tipped with a smidgen of the singsong poetic, but with the childlike exuberance of posing a dare.

Chad took Maylee's hand in his. They continued their walk around the lake.

The swim across the lake and back was under half a mile. Chad and Maylee swam side by side, stroke for stroke. It was refreshing after having worked up a sweat from walking around the lake.

When they came out of the water, Maylee in her one-piece bathing suit, Chad in his trunks, Cara handed each a towel. "Wow," she said, "you two are putting Monty and me to shame."

"No shame here," Monty said, sitting atop the picnic table, his feet on the bench. He stood and raised his hand over his head, his fingers interlaced, and stretched. "Breakfast, anyone?"

"I'm starving," Chad said as he patted his torso dry.

"I know a good breakfast diner not far," Maylee said as she draped her towel across her shoulder.

"Then on to Yosemite," Cara volunteered. "Agreed?"

In a quicksilver moment, a glint of hesitation washed over Monty's face.

"Sounds good to me," Chad said.

"What are we waiting for?" Monty said in a ringing voice, but his eyes told a different story than his words. It was clear he was trying to decide: *Run or stay?*

Was Monty worried about getting burned again after his recent divorce? Before Sandy, Monty never had a qualm. "Love 'em and leave 'em" was his mantra back in the day, when the two of them were at their carousing peak, meeting women in bars with their roguish act of wit and charm.

Monty and Chad had been like a well-oiled machine, each adding a bon mot to the other's words, acting as straight man to the other's comedic lines. They were interchangeable, each feeding off the other, each wooing and seducing.

They were like adventurers who, after a conquest and the subsequent dates, left the young lovelies high and dry, some of whom had fallen in love. Phone calls stopped, and when the woman called to see what was up, they put them off with a patented excuse about work. For Chad, "I am heading to Montana to film a movie. Not sure when I'll be back" was a variation of the standard "It's over" line.

Some of the women took it in stride; others were hurt by the sudden break. Over the years, Chad had run into some of his former flings, and often they ignored him as though not knowing him, but one woman blasted him an earful at a local hangout in Sherman Oaks.

"Well, well, if it isn't Mr. Phony-Baloney," she said in a sharp, clipped tone when Chad bumped into her at the bar. She was sitting on a stool with a girlfriend, who, if Chad remembered correctly, had hooked up with Monty on the night they all had met.

"Look," Chad said as he motioned to get the bartender's attention, "I—"

The woman cut in. "Save it," she snapped. She turned her back on Chad and began a conversation with her friend.

Chad wasn't proud of his treatment of women, but he had not lost any sleep over it. He had experienced the bitter sting of rejection when Monica, the beauty on the *Gunsmoke* set, had left him high and dry. That was a bewildering, painful experience, but he recovered, or so he told himself. He did not want to dwell on the possibility that Monica's rejection had turned him into a coldhearted cad.

But now with Maylee, Chad had no desire to abandon the romance, no desire to run. He wanted to be with her, to listen to her, to learn from her. But was he certain she felt the same way as he? Heading to the tent to change, he told himself not to overthink it.

CHAPTER 9

AFTER A BREAKFAST OF PANCAKES all around, they hit the road, departing the diner, with Cara driving and Monty riding shotgun. Monty had offered the seat to Maylee, but she had said the back was fine with her.

"I have a request," Monty said to Cara, before turning to Maylee, who was sitting behind the driver's seat and across from Chad. "I am looking forward to Yosemite, but might we sleep in real beds tonight?"

"Are you a Mr. Softy too?" Cara said, glancing over her shoulder to Chad.

"A bed would be nice," Chad said with a lift of his shoulders, his gaze on Maylee.

"What do you say, Maylee?" Cara said.

"Bed," she replied in a tone suggesting she was in on a gag.

"Beds it is," Cara said as she eased over into the right lane and onto an exit ramp for I-680 North. She tilted her head toward Monty while keeping her eyes on the road. "Would not want Sir Monty escaping on us."

Monty flashed an open-mouthed look at Cara, the expression of one who had met his match.

Maylee suggested they try the Evergreen Lodge. "It has hiking trails, a pool, a restaurant, and," she said with a ringmaster's trill in her voice, "a tavern for wayward travelers."

"All right," Cara said, "now that we have that settled, what say we all pay equal shares of the rent. Two days sound about right?"

Monty said over his shoulder, "What say to independent woman, old chap?"

"I like it." Chad grinned at Maylee, who smiled her approval.

Monty suggested they stop and call to make sure there were vacancies, but Cara made a *pshh* sound, accompanied by a dismissive wave. "*Spontaneity* is the order of the day."

They were in luck: the Evergreen Lodge had vacancies. Each couple took a one-bedroom cabin with a kitchen, a stone fireplace, and a patio with a view of a towering pine forest.

They decided on lunch at the sundeck off the restaurant, which was situated in the center of the twenty-acre property.

"This place has a rustic beauty that I find appealing," Monty said.

"We are in the Sierra Nevada range." Maylee lifted a finger as though to say, *One more thing.* "This location was originally built for workers building the O'Shaughnessy Dam in Hetch Hetchy Valley."

"Hetch Hetchy?" Monty said.

"The name is derived from the Miwok word *hetchetci*—'het chet chee,'" Maylee enunciated, "describing seeds from a prominent grass growing in the valley and from which a mush was made."

"Let me guess," Chad said. "You wrote a story about the dam."

"No," Maylee said, "I stayed here while I wrote a story about Yosemite and John Muir, who was instrumental in keeping livestock out of the area and getting it designated as a national park."

A waitress came over to the table to hand out menus and ask for drink orders.

"Before you consider a libation, Sir Monty," Cara said, her eyes dancing with mischief, "I know a wonderful trail we should all hike after lunch."

"This woman is always one step ahead of me," Monty said to Chad. He looked at the young woman server, who smiled and raised her brow in a touché at Monty. "Water neat, please." He made a face at Cara: *Good?*

She smirked at him and ordered an iced tea.

While they studied their menus, Chad said to Maylee, "You seem to retain the minutiae of research for articles."

"Maylee," Cara said, looking over her menu, with a note of pride in her voice, "has a photographic memory."

"Really?" Monty said as the waitress returned with their drinks.

They ordered. After Monty returned his menu to the waitress, he focused on Maylee as though unsure. "Reel-leee," he repeated, but this time with emphasis as he dragged the word out.

"You are full of surprises," Chad said to Maylee.

"Surprises, you say?" Maylee said in her singsong voice.

"Yes." Monty laughed. "Incoming."

Maylee folded her hands on the edge of the table and began: "Surprise is a feeling, / Arriving so quick. / But will it remain, / Or vanish in a click? / Time will tell / As it always will. / Revealing the truth / When the mind is still."

They hiked in Mariposa Grove, a forest of giant sequoias. The width and height of the massive trees was breathtaking. The trail was wide. There were other hikers and some groups of schoolchildren on guided tours.

They saw a tunnel running through a sequoia tree. When Monty asked why it was that way, of course, Maylee explained, "It was done way back when, to allow coaches to pass through as a marketing scheme. There's another one farther down."

Down a ways, they came to an enormous sequoia. "That tree is called the Grizzly Giant. It's one of the largest and oldest trees in the world—been here over two thousand years."

"I wonder how tall?" Chad said with the intent of testing Maylee's knowledge.

"Two hundred and two feet," she replied.

"Like having a walking encyclopedia," Monty said as they walked two abreast through the second tree tunnel.

"Mayleepedia, as in encyclopedia," Chad said.

"I like that," Cara said. "Mayleepedia, the all-knowing."

They came to a group of four trees, three of them growing close together, with the fourth a little more distant.

"Isn't that something?" Monty said. "It's like they are four trees in one."

"The Bachelor and Three Graces," Maylee said. "Their roots are so intertwined that if one were to fall, it would likely bring the others along."

The hike took over two hours, the last mile of which was up a steep incline.

As Monty opened the sliding door to the VW bus, he said to Maylee, "Madam Guide, please do us the honor of sitting up front."

As they piled inside the vehicle, Chad said to Monty, "In need of a snooze, are we?"

Monty stretched out in the back, feet toward the rear, his head resting on seat cushion. "I am going to dream of the cold libations I have earned after that strenuous walkabout."

"Cara," Chad said, "I bet you and your girlfriend did not find that little stroll in the woods strenuous."

Cara was driving out of the parking lot. Shafts of sunlight peeking through the trees were lighting up the windshield.

Cara glanced at Maylee, who said, "Incoming."

"We're listening," Chad said with eager anticipation.

"Look up and listen. Can you hear? / Here come they, over beyond the far hill, / On their galloping steeds. / Gentlemen riders, or so they claim, / Their metallic suits shining in the sunlight. / Lost boys *they* are, fighting the wrong fight, / But oh so beautiful in their quest for the light, / As they cull the slayed dragon in their mind, / As they cull the slayed dragons in their mind."

It came over Chad that the perception of this woman, whom he had known for only a few days, through her insightful poems not only was accurate but also had triggered a stirring, a wanting.

Back at the lodge, Cara and Maylee decided on a late afternoon swim.

After showering, Chad changed into jeans, a long-sleeved T-shirt, and a flannel shirt that he wore untucked. He went to Monty's room and found him on his patio.

Chad, noticing that there were two wicker chairs, took a seat next to his friend, who had a can of beer in his hand.

Monty lifted his beer. "I bought a six-pack. In the fridge if you are so inclined."

"I'll wait for the tavern."

"This place has it all," Monty said as he gazed at the nearby woodlands, a patch of wild grass lying between, "knickknack slash general store, restaurant, tavern ..."

"Don't forget beautiful female artist who has you figured out."

Monty took a swig of his beer. "Yeah," he said, tapping his knuckles on a circular side table between them, "she is something else."

"So, you are okay with continuing this road trip?"

"Is that what this is?"

"Not sure what *it* is." Chad leaned forward, his hand on his knee. "But I am in no hurry to end it."

"Yeah," Monty said, "I got a little gun-shy so close to the divorce and all—"

"But," Chad cut in, "Cara read you like a book and called you on it."

"Yup." Monty ran his finger around the rim of his beer can and took a sip. "Something about her is always one step—"

"Sheeet," Chad cut in with a lift of his brow and a glimmer of disbelief in his eyes. "Let us not forget the fact that she is gorgeous, which always keeps you in the game 'til—"

"Wait a minute, Mr. I Have Never Taken the Plunge. I once actually went all the way and got married."

"How did that work out for you?"

"Low blow," Monty said through a self-deprecating laugh. He jabbed his index finger at Chad. "Maylee has cast a spell on you, my friend." He jutted his jaw at Chad, his eyes saying, *Am I not right?*

"No doubt," Chad said. "No doubt."

"Funny," Monty said, "that it would be …" He waved his hand in the air.

"A nice-enough-looking but unglamorous woman," Chad said. He extended his hand to make a point. "But since I've gotten to know her, that beautiful mind has transformed her from the undesirable plain Jane to Maylee the desirable. It's as though I can't get enough of her."

Monty laughed a soft, deep chuckle with a tone of approval to it. "Who knew that the one to capture your heart would be the opposite of every woman I have ever seen you with?

"Question," Monty said, standing. "Where will you and I be in a year?" He lifted a finger to indicate *Just a second* and went inside and returned with a fresh beer.

Monty popped open his beer and sat. "What do you think?"

"I think," Chad said as he heard the front door open, "that we have seen our last Chad-and-Monty one-on-one road trip."

Cara and Maylee came out to the patio in their bathing suits. Golden Cara, her body tucked in her bikini like a glove, looked ravenously beautiful. Maylee's appeal was more subtle, not with the outgoing vibrancy of Cara, but more with the reserved inner beauty of a wise fairy-tale princess.

"There they are, our providers of sustenance and much-needed libations," Cara said in a voice ringing with good cheer. "Our knights in shining armor—Sir Monty and Sir Chad."

"To the tavern, fair maidens," Monty said with a bow of his head and forward roll of his hand in front of his face.

Chad stood. "Lady Maylee and I shall visit our changing station and join you at the appointed waystation at five bells." He looked at Maylee, who nodded her approval. He then took her by the hand and led her to the door.

The tavern was a comfortable-looking space with hardwood floors, shiplap walls adorned with paintings of cattle drives and mountain vistas, wooden bench booths, and a long bar, behind which was a plateglass mirror.

"Let's take that empty corner," Monty said, eyeing the nearly empty bar.

"We're having luck with bar corners," Chad said.

"And other things." Cara lifted her brow toward Chad, a pleasant I-know-what-you-did-last-night glimmer emerging.

As the women sat on each side of the corner bar, the guys standing between them, Chad glanced at Maylee, who had assumed the expression of one slightly bemused.

The women ordered wine; the men, beer.

"Suggestion for tomorrow," Monty said as the drinks arrived.

"This ought to be good," Chad said. He slid a white wine to Cara and a red to Maylee.

Monty wrapped his fingers around his sixteen-ounce beer mug and took a long swallow.

"Well?" Chad said.

Monty lifted a hand to Chad as if to say, *Patience.* "It would be sin to come so close to Yosemite National Park and not see it." He leaned his shoulder into Chad's. "I say that we allow Maylee to guide us. Does not my good friend agree?"

Chad cradled his beer mug, lifted it, and took a long, thirsty swallow. "Good beer," he said. He tapped the bar with his fist. "Cara, whatever have you done to Monty?"

CHAPTER 10

A T YOSEMITE FALLS, MAYLEE SAID, "It's a seven-mile hike. Are we all good with that?" She eyed Monty.

Monty nodded his approval as he took in the rock formations, the woodlands in the distance, and of course the falls, the water cascading into the lake. He asked if the falls fell year-round.

"No," Maylee replied. "We are witnessing the full force of the three falls because of the spring melt."

The hike took five hours, but Chad found it worth every strenuous climb. The sights were spectacular. Though something had changed with Maylee. Twice during the walk, he took her hand in his, but each time, within a minute, she had released her grip. And last night when they turned in, she had given Chad a peck on the cheek and said good night, rolling over on her side away from him.

After the hike, on the way out of the park, Maylee drew their attention to a few points of interest. "El Capitan," she said, pointing to a crag of a mountain, "is popular with mountain climbers and is almost entirely made of granite."

Though she sounded and looked the same, Chad had an uneasy feeling. Was she regretting the other night of passion? Was she possibly concerned that things were happening too quickly? Was their sharing of a cabin bringing on a one-to-one intimacy much too soon? All three were possibly true to varying degrees. When she considered them all, did it give her pause?

When Chad and Maylee returned to their room at the lodge, he considered asking her if everything was okay between them, but decided against it, fearing he may not like her response.

The phone on the nightstand in the bedroom rang. Maylee rushed to answer it.

"Hello," she said into the receiver. "Yes. This is she."

For a long half minute, Maylee sat on the side of the bed listening, an expression of impending doom on her face. "I see," she said in a defeated voice. "I will be there tomorrow."

"What's going on?"

"Let's go to dinner and I will explain to everyone."

Chad recalled a particular part of the poem Maylee had recited when they stood before the Ansel Adams photograph *Lodgepole Pines* at the Monterey Museum of Art that highlighted the contrast between darkness and light: "But if I soared high above the shadow and glow, / Will I still maintain my eternal flow?"

Change was in the air.

At a booth in the tavern, Maylee said to the group, "I must leave for Barstow in the morning."

"Your mother?" Cara asked.

"Yes," Maylee replied. "She's been put in hospice care at a nursing home."

"I will take you," Chad said.

Maylee tipped her head as though to assure herself she had heard correctly.

"I insist, Maylee," Chad said.

"Very well," Maylee replied. She excused herself again. "I need to make another call."

After Maylee left, Chad directed a strong beam of attention at Cara.

"Her mother has been sick for a while now—lung cancer," Cara said. She took a sip of her wine and brought her fist up under her chin, her lips pursed.

"You can trust Chad," Monty said. "But I think you already know that."

"I do." She went on to reveal that over the last year, Maylee had made several trips back to Barstow to see her mother, "Who is a fiercely independent woman. She did not want her daughter moving back to Barstow. Her mother is so proud that her daughter is a writer and did not want her failing health to be a drag on her career."

The waitress came to the table with menus. Chad thanked her and said they would need a few minutes. He returned his attention to Cara.

Cara said, "Maylee has been checking in with a woman who worked at the diner with her mother. This woman looked in on her every day, since her mother would never let Maylee know she was in a bad way. I suggested this trip up the coast to get her mind off things for a while."

Chad couldn't believe that Maylee had not shared any of this with him, that their relationship was not what he thought it was. Possibly she didn't want to burden Chad with her woe and upset their romance, or maybe their *romance* was just a diversion, a hiatus from the reality of her life.

Maylee returned to the table. "This being our last night," she said with a spirited lift in her voice, "let us enjoy the company of each other, for who knows when we will once again be together." She scanned the table for concurrence, her gaze settling on Chad.

"I have a true story about a famous actor." Chad lifted his brow to Maylee: *Okay?*

Maylee said yes with her eyes, and Chad mentioned he'd had a small part in a John Wayne movie, *The Cowboys*. "Where Bruce Dern is the villain and kills the Duke's character, which didn't happen often." Chad glanced at Maylee to check if this was something she wanted to hear.

"Nobody plays a bad hombre better than Bruce Dern." Maylee lifted her brow as though to say, *Please continue.*

"Bruce Dern and John Wayne did not particularly get along," Chad said, his mind flashing back to one of his first jobs in movies, "and the Duke wasn't one bit happy about his character getting killed by him."

"Let me guess," Monty interjected, "the Duke—"

Chad interrupted, "You know the story, wise guy." He looked at Monty as though to say, *Really?*

"Oh," Monty said through a guilty smile. "So I do. Please continue."

"Well, sir," Chad said, his voice taking on a storyteller's folksy twang, "the afternoon before the Duke's demise, Dern and Slim Pickens were having a drink with the big man in his trailer." Chad leaned forward, his eyes wide, his mouth slightly open. "Next thing, the door to the trailer opens and Dern comes flying out, landing in a heap, still in desperado costume—buckskin coat, bandanna around the neck, gun belt on waist."

Chad checked the table. Cara and Maylee were both listening intently. Monty had the expression of one who knew the ending but still wanted to hear.

"Then," Chad said, making a stiff gesture with his hand, "the Duke storms out of the trailer and lifts Dern off the ground and brings him in real close, face-to-face." Chad paused for effect.

"And?" Maylee asked.

"The Duke says, 'Pilgrim, you rub me the goddamn wrong way.' He then tossed old Bruce to the ground like he was a rag doll. You could have heard a pin drop on the set."

"Pilgrim?" Maylee said, slanting a dubious look at Chad.

"I swear," Chad said, hand raised. "He called him Pilgrim."

"Tell them about the next day on the set, Chad," Monty said.

"In the film, Bruce Dern's character and the Duke get in a fistfight before Dern shoots the Duke in the back, killing his character." Chad shook his head at the memory and laughed. "When it was all over, the Duke was dead, but not before he had cracked Dern's rib and administered a purple bruise under his eye, in the most real fake fistfight I have ever seen—no stuntmen for this scene. The Duke insisted."

And so the evening progressed over a round of drinks and dinner. From time to time, Chad tried to assure himself that Maylee was back to normal and that he had misinterpreted things—but his gut told him otherwise.

Monty told a story about selling Lucille Ball's house. "In Spaulding Square neighborhood after she passed away. Her daughter, Lucie Arnaz, represented the family, and after the sale went down, Lucie took me to lunch at the Brown Derby to celebrate, in her mother's 1967 royal-blue Mercedes-Benz convertible."

Monty smiled at the memory. "I told Lucie she should call the car 'the Lucie Mobile.'"

"And," Cara inquired, "did she call it the Lucie Mobile?"

"I like to think so," Monty said.

After a round of after-dinner drinks were ordered, Cara said, "Well, since we're name-dropping, I once sold a painting of Bob Hope to his wife."

"Go on with you," Monty said.

"It's true," Maylee said. "I was with her when she delivered it to their house."

"Was it a portrait?" Chad asked as the drinks arrived.

"No," Cara said. She took a sip of her wine and smiled her approval. "It was of him entertaining the troops during the war—World War Two—and I drew it off a photograph Mrs. Hope had given me."

"It reminded me of a Norman Rockwell." Maylee grabbed Chad's wrist and said, "My good friend is a multitalented artist."

"Your turn, Maylee," Monty said with a nod of encouragement.

"Wee-lll," she said, stretching the word out as though considering, "I don't have any stories about famous people, but I just called my agent and my novel has been accepted by Random House."

"What!" Chad exclaimed. It crossed his mind that most people would have broadcast this huge bit of news immediately, but not Maylee.

After congratulations all around, Maylee said, "If ever a moment called for a poem.

"So bitter, so sweet, / Is the Fates' favorite play / In finding my true calling, / Though at rest my meemaw will soon lay. / O the journey is not for the faint, / But I would have it no other way, / For in the end, / We are all children in a play."

After dinner, all four returned to Monty and Cara's cabin. Monty suggested they sit out on the patio.

"Monty, shall we take a couple of chairs outside?" Chad motioned toward the dining room table with its four chairs.

Cara and Maylee sat in the wicker chairs, the guys sitting across from each other at an angle so that the women were in their view.

Chad glanced at the woodlands, which was in shadowy outline, as darkness had fallen. "I will rent a car tomorrow," he said to the group, who were all visible, but the fine details of their features were hidden by the darkness.

"How about," Monty said, leaning forward in his chair, his forearms on his thighs, his hands folded together, "I buy one of those cellular mobile phones, and that way we can stay in touch?" He looked at Maylee as if to say, *What do you think?*

Maylee was sitting erect as though a rod had been inserted in her spine. "That is fine," she said in a tentative voice. The good cheer of the tavern conversations had left her as the raw reality of her mother's situation hung over her. "With my mother being in hospice, I don't know how long I—"

"How long *we* will be there," Chad said, with emphasis on the word *we*.

"After," Maylee said, as she lifted her eyes toward the woods, a pale moon slipping out from behind a dark cloud, spilling light over the tops of the pine trees, "we must reconnect."

The following morning, Monty and Chad went out and returned to the cabin with a cellular phone and a rental car.

Over a late breakfast at the lodge restaurant, the details were worked out. Monty and Cara would head toward the Pacific Northwest in the van. "With you always on my mind," Cara said to Maylee.

Chad and Maylee planned to visit her mother at the nursing home first. "We'll take one last look at my mother's trailer—the same one I grew up in," she said. Chad or Maylee would call when there was any news to report.

After checking out, they went to their respective vehicles, which were parked in front of the cabins. There were hugs all around, signaling the end of something special.

"Keep me posted, Maylee," Cara said with a wave as she opened the passenger's-side door to the van. And then they were off, the VW heading north, the rental car south.

CHAPTER 11

The drive to Barstow was five hours, Maylee told Chad, as she pointed to an exit sign for US 355 South. "Basically just follow the signs to Barstow," she said.

They were in a 1994 Buick LeSabre sedan, a car Monty would have never rented, but it suited Chad just fine. It rode smooth, and the bench seat provided plenty of legroom.

"If you are tired," Chad said, "go ahead and take a nap."

"I am tired. Didn't sleep much last night," Maylee said. "But I don't think sleep is an option."

She folded her arms across her chest, her gaze on Chad. "Thank for you for doing this," she said, releasing a hand from the fold and, in a short sweep, indicating renting the car, before returning her hand to its folded position. "And for ..." Maylee's voice trailed off into a heavy sigh.

Chad took his right hand off the steering wheel and used it to reach for her hand. "If you want to talk," he said, giving a gentle squeeze, "I am a good listener."

Maylee nodded as though considering the offer. She looked out her window. "We are driving out of a glacier-carved valley."

"Long time ago," Chad said, approaching, on his left, a rugged rock formation along a hillside.

"You know what William Blake said about time?" Maylee asked.

"'Hold infinity in the palm of your hand and eternity in an hour.'"

"Very good," she said.

"The poem you said to me back at the lake in San Jose, you mentioned time and eternity," Chad said as he lifted his finger toward an overhead sign indicating CA 58 East, showing that the Barstow exit was coming up in one mile.

"Yes," Maylee said. "And yes, I pilfer sometimes in my writing." She began to yawn. Covering her mouth with the back of her wrist, she went on through the yawn. "But remember," she said with the lift of a cautionary finger, "I do not steal whole ideas, just tidbits here and there to help me along."

"Same with acting," Chad said as he checked the rearview mirror and moved into the exit lane. "When I watch a movie, I am always looking for ..." He fluttered his hand in the air in search of the right words.

"Facial expressions and delivery of lines—not the words per se, but the way they are spoken," Maylee said.

"Exactly," Chad said as he veered into the right lane of the exit ramp and stopped to wait for a break in traffic. Ahead, across the highway, was a field of green and yellow wildflowers, beyond which were cinnamon hills.

They drove on in silence. After a while, Maylee looked around as if reorienting herself. She took a breath as if to say, *Here goes.* "My mother had me when she was seventeen years old, and though she was not a perfect mother, she sacrificed her life for the life I now live."

She stared straight ahead as though boring through the changed landscape, from the rugged mountains of Yosemite to the high desert teeming with creosote bush, high chaparral, and a variety of desert shrubs.

Chad did a mathematical calculation and determined that Maylee's mother was in her midfifties—less than ten years older than he. "Tell me about your mom."

"When she was younger, my mother was the type of woman whom men found desirable. Not exactly pretty, but she possessed a certain willowy appeal." Maylee sighed, her face blanketed by fatigue. "And she was smart, not book smart, but survival smart."

Maylee's mouth got small, strained, as she absentmindedly examined her fingernails, which were clear and neatly trimmed. "After my father left," she said, lifting her gaze to Chad, "my mother drank daily, sometimes passing out on the sofa. She smoked like a chimney and went out with the wrong men, sometimes leaving her ten-year-old daughter alone in a trailer park overnight."

Maylee motioned to an exit sign. "Take exit 183." She gave her head a little shake. "By the time I was twelve, I knew that whatever it took, I was leaving Barstow and the world of trailer parks."

Chad drove onto the exit ramp and said, "And look at what you have accomplished—graduate of Cal, writer, poet, and soon-to-be published author, with Random House no less."

Maylee set her gaze on Chad as though considering, then a crunched, focused expression came over her face. "Take a right, and then a mile down the road take a left at the traffic light," she said in a weary yet direct voice.

The nursing home was on the outskirts of Barstow, a two-story L-shaped complex. From the outside, everything appeared neat and orderly. The parking lot was spotless, and the light gray siding on the exterior of the nursing home was sparkling clean.

Chad pulled into a parking space and turned off the engine. "Maylee, take as much time as you need."

She took a deep breath and exhaled. "Okay," she said in a hurried voice. She then exited the car and headed for the front door.

After Maylee entered the building, Chad got out and stretched. He had never been to Barstow, though some of his acting colleagues had been on location nearby. He could understand why the site was sometimes selected: it had little rain, and the high desert with its desolate vastness provided a moody atmosphere.

In Chad's mind, good acting and good writing were obviously critical to the making of a successful film, but location could make a good movie a great movie. *The Treasure of the Sierra Madre* was a prime example. Humphrey Bogart, Walter Huston, and the rest of the cast were great, but the primitive and harsh desert location not only complemented the desperateness of the characters but also took the movie to the level of greatness. It was as though the desert and the wind were characters too.

The air was dry and arid. A bit of a breeze ruffled a US flag, below which was a flag for the state of California—with a grizzly bear on the prowl—attached to a flagpole stationed in a green in the middle of a circular drive that arced around the front of the building. Chad felt like taking a walk, but he got back into the car, not wanting to wander too far, in case Maylee returned.

Sensing that there was more to her story about growing up, he wondered if it would be revealed in her novel *Desert Girl*. He was curious to read the manuscript but did not want to push the issue. It might even make a good movie—and the author might put in a good word for a part. What part exactly would Chad play? Other than a brief history of her childhood and a cursory revelation of her love life, Chad knew little about her.

And Maylee had incomplete knowledge of his life. Yes, he had told of his childhood and career, and he had acknowledged Cara and Maylee's deduction that he and Monty had been carousing womanizers, though that did not seem to bother either woman outwardly. But sometime down the road as the relationship progressed, Maylee might hold it against him and view him as someone not to be trusted.

But she didn't know that on the movie set, he treated everyone with respect and never made an advance toward a woman during filming. And Maylee didn't know that he would never, ever cheat on her—never.

Some actors and directors did take advantage on a movie set, which was something that Chad found repulsive. He knew that he was not in a good defense of this stance, with his and Monty's "love 'em and leave 'em" ways, but rightly or wrongly he considered that in a social setting the women were under no obligation to give in to his advances. But a star actor or director had undue power over an actress, especially young actresses with no clout.

Maylee approached the car. In her gray pullover sweater-shirt, dark slacks, and ankle-high sneakers, she moved with effortless coordination, her arms swinging in rhythm, her stride quick.

"Mama would like to meet you," she said, bending down to the open driver's-side window.

A little scrabble of panic shot through Chad. "Oh."

"She told me that any man who would drive me all this way was someone she needed to see before …" Maylee drew in her bottom lip, a question in her eyes.

"Well then, let's go meet Mama." Chad opened the door and headed toward the entrance with Maylee at his side.

The nursing home had an antiseptic hospital smell that always made Chad uncomfortable. The patients were elderly, all at varying degrees of nearness to death's door. A large room off the main lobby had a television blaring a game show, with old folks sitting at a table or in wheelchairs, some watching television, others staring into space.

An orderly in starched whites pushed a withered old man down a corridor. The old gent's head drooped to his shoulder, his gaze utterly vacant as though his mind had already deserted him.

As Chad passed, the elderly man's eyes sprung open, staring at Chad. "I used to be somebody in World War Two," he croaked wistfully.

Past the front desk, Maylee led Chad to room 113, inside of which was a shriveled-up woman propped up in bed with the head portion raised. There was a tube attached to her nose and another tube running from her arm to a heart monitor, which was blinking numbers.

Maylee's mother took in her approaching daughter but seemed not to recognize her for a moment.

"Ah, hello, Daughter. So good of you to come."

Maylee and Chad stood bedside. "Mama, this is Chad."

"Who?"

"The man who drove me here and whom you told me you wanted to meet."

"Oh." Mama grunted. "Yes, now I remember." She offered a thin, veiny hand, the skin gray and sickly looking. "Eunice Lee here. So nice to meet you."

Chad took her hand, which was ice-cold and clammy. "Hello, Eunice."

Eunice turned Chad's hand over. She strained to lean forward and examined his palm, running a finger from the heel to the base of his index finger—exactly like Maylee had done.

"Long lifeline," she said. "Might have yourself a keeper, Daughter."

A thin catlike smile came over Eunice's face, and for a brief moment Chad saw the comely young woman she once was: a hardscrabble woman who possessed a certain female allure that would have drawn the fancy of many a blue-collar fellow.

Eunice released his hand and sat back in bed, her eyes on Chad as though taking stock of him. "If I had met a man like you when my daughter was young, I would not be in here today." She raised her brow toward Maylee and said, "Men can be the ruination or the salvation of many a woman."

She flashed a hard look at Maylee and shifted her gaze to Chad. "She would look much prettier if she would get rid of those god-awful glasses, don't you think?"

A tap on the door signaled the entrance of a nurse, who came in with a bustle and whose consumption of space indicated she was in charge. She was a big-boned woman somewhere between fifty and sixty years of age and had the seen-it-all demeanor of an experienced medical professional.

While the nurse checked over Eunice, Maylee and Chad sat in oversized vinyl chairs, facing the foot of Eunice's bed.

"All right then," the nurse said in a tone indicating the completion of her task. At the door, the nurse said in a low voice to Maylee, "I would like a word in the hallway."

"Be right there." Maylee stood and went to her mother.

Eunice said, "I hate this place. I. Want. To. Die." There was now force in her voice, a determination. She closed her eyes and tipped her head to the side as a tear streaked down her cheek.

"Oh, Mama." Maylee bent over her mother, putting her hand on her shoulder.

Eunice shot a withering look at Chad, who was still seated. "Who is that?"

Maylee kissed her mother on the cheek and said, "Get some rest, Mama. I will be here when you awake."

"If," Eunice said, "I have my way"—she drew in a raspy breath, her lips trembling—"then I will ... not ... wake up." Her mouth gaped opened, revealing a missing incisor and thin purple gums.

Maylee asked Chad to wait in the room while she went to talk to the nurse.

While Eunice lay still, only an occasional wheeze indicated that she was still alive. Chad thought about his parents, who were old enough to be Eunice's parents. Chad's father was seventy-eight; his mother, seventy-seven. Both were in reasonably good health, with a few issues. Dad had high blood pressure and Mom arthritis, but both still drove and lived in the same house Chad and his sisters had grown up in. Both sisters lived nearby and looked in on the parents.

Chad's father had mellowed some over the years, especially after he retired at age sixty-five. Chad usually called home once a week. If his father answered, the conversation was brief. Then he'd hear, "I'll get your mother. Delores! Chad on the phone."

There was still that impenetrable distance between father and son—that silent wall. Never in his life had Richard Carson spoken the words "I love you" to his son. Never even came close.

It was with his mother that Chad had a bond. Their conversations were free and easy, his mom asking about his career or mentioning how a neighbor had complimented his performance in a movie. She was proud of her son's career and insisted that her husband join her in watching his performances on television or in the theater. Chad wasn't sure what his father thought of his acting career.

Last Christmas, Chad went home. Over a couple of beers at his dad's local tavern, Richard said he had enjoyed a film Chad had a supporting part in. He never mentioned Chad's performance, which was par for the course. So, there it was, not a terrible relationship with his father, but not a true bond either. It was as though they were acquaintances and not blood relatives.

Had Chad now reached a point in his life where he needed to bond with a partner to share in each other's life? He had been with many a woman in the past, but none drew him like Maylee. Was it her unique characteristics alone, or was it also that he was at a stage in his life where he was tired of being alone, tired of the same old, same old? He felt that Maylee had come at the right time in his life to alter the course of, not only his rededication to his career, but also his life's journey. But did she feel the same way? Her novel had been accepted by Random House, which was like Chad perhaps getting the lead in a major film—a life-altering event. He saw the irony between now and when they had first met, when Chad had been the unsure one. But now it seemed to be the other way around.

Chad snapped out of his reverie and saw Eunice staring at him, a confused expression on her face. "I'm Chad," he said. "Your daughter's friend."

Eunice, from her prone position, one hand atop the other with both of them resting on her stomach, eyeballed Chad with the same vacant look he'd seen in the eyes of the old man being pushed down the corridor by the orderly.

"I was once young and pretty," she said in a wheezy voice, which sounded just a bit like Maylee's poetry cadence. "A whole life ahead of me," she continued through a croupy cough. "And then it all changed with one mistake." She hacked a cough and then another, her face brightening in a purplish hue.

Chad, fearing she might be nearing the end, was ready to get help, when the door opened and Maylee entered.

"Oh, Mama," Maylee said, rushing to her mother's bedside.

Chad got out of his chair, tapped Maylee on the shoulder as she held her mother's hand, and said, "I'll wait outside for you."

There were chairs in the main lobby, but Chad was uncomfortable sitting there in this controlled menagerie for the elderly. So, over the next two hours he waited in the car, with intervals of returning to the lobby and checking for Maylee.

On his fifth return, Chad spotted Maylee at the front desk. She was holding a folder of paperwork and talking to a man in a suit, an administrator of some sort, Chad surmised.

The door to Eunice's room opened. Out came two orderlies, pushing a gurney into the corridor, a sheet covering what must have been Eunice's body.

Maylee watched the gurney as it was wheeled down the corridor, until it disappeared around a corner. She said something to the administrator and then headed toward the front door, when she recognized Chad standing off to the side.

She came up to Chad, her expression vulnerable, like a fawn lost in a forest. She opened the folder and took out a bankbook and a folded sheet of white paper, which she unfolded. "My mother's will and," she said, waving the bankbook, "her net worth of one hundred fifty-one dollars and thirty-one cents."

"Come on," Chad said softly. "Let me take you out of here."

CHAPTER 12

O N THE WAY TO EUNICE'S trailer, Maylee told Chad that she was having her mother's body cremated. "It was in her hand-scrawled will. Also, she wanted no funeral service of any kind."

Maylee then told Chad to take a left at the upcoming traffic light.

He came to a stop at the red arrow and said, "Nothing?"

"I'm going to settle up with the rental office at the trailer park, and then tomorrow afternoon I would like to pick up my mother's ashes at the funeral home." She looked at Chad as though seeking his okay before continuing.

"Yes," Chad replied.

"And the following morning spread my mother's ashes at a certain location. If this is too—"

"I am good with it, Maylee."

The light turned green. They rode in silence other than Maylee giving directions.

Chad imagined Maylee was reliving her time in Barstow, her time with her mother, and possibly her escape from Barstow into a life of successful independence—a journey that must have been more difficult for a woman, a journey possibly haunted by difficulties from the past.

"Turn left onto the gravel road up ahead," Maylee said.

Chad saw a neon sign atop a metal pole, advertising Desert Oasis Trailer Park. They were on the other side of town from the nursing home, past an industrial park of chain-link fences and warehouses.

Maylee directed Chad to park in front of a weather-beaten vinyl trailer. "I want one last look before I go to the rental office," she said.

Entering the trailer, Chad smelled the strong odor of cigarette smoke intermingled with a lingering faint smell of cheap liquor and stale food. It brought to mind a dive bar the morning after.

"Welcome to my wonder years," Maylee said as they stood at the door, taking in the sight before them: the lime-green walls splotched with yellow discoloration, dirty dishes piled high in the sink, empty liquor bottles in a cardboard box in a corner.

"Huh," Maylee said as she stepped toward an L-shaped bench and its accompanying Formica table with a tattered album book resting atop it.

Maylee slid into the bench seat. Atop the album was an envelope, which she opened. "It's from my mother." She displayed a sheet of plain white paper with one side crammed with scrawled handwriting in blue ink.

After poring over the letter, Maylee stared at it for a beat before looking over at Chad, who was leaning against the kitchen countertop, waiting for her next move.

Maylee opened the album. Her mouth gaped open. While keeping her eyes on the page, she said to Chad, "Would you come over?"

Chad sat next to her and saw four black-and-white photographs of a teenaged girl and an infant. One photo was of the girl feeding the baby a bottle; another, of the baby lying on her back, staring at the camera with a querulous look; another, of the girl holding the baby; and lastly, of the baby asleep on her back. At the bottom of the page was written, "Baby Mary, two weeks."

"I've never seen this album before." Maylee turned the page. "Oh my," she said as she came upon more pictures of herself as an infant.

She scrolled through the album until she came to the last page, where she saw a picture of one-year-old baby Mary standing with a tentative smile, as if to say, *I think I can.* Written below was "Mary's first step."

Maylee exhaled and placed her elbows on the table, her fingers spread over her eyebrows.

Chad remained quiet, wanting to allow Maylee time to digest what she had seen.

"I think," Maylee said, closing the album, "there is a part of my mother that I will never understand." She tapped the letter. "My mother stowed the album away, and"—she lifted the letter and read—"'I simply forgot about it after the bad times began with your father.'"

Maylee shook her head. "I don't believe that." She fixed her eyes on Chad. "Why would she hide this from me—why?" Maylee waved her hands as though to say, *Forget it.* "Let's get out of here," she said as she grabbed the album and slid out of the bench seat.

Departing the trailer, Chad thought that his childhood looked pretty good at this moment. He was now seeing that his father was like a saint in comparison to Maylee's. Yes, Richard Carson was distant, but he never deserted his family. He provided Chad and his siblings a roof to live under and food on the table, all the while fighting the demons of a world war.

At the rental office, Maylee arranged to have her mother's trailer cleaned and sold. The rental office would get a percent of the sale. On the way to the car, she asked Chad, "Are you sure you are okay with the next couple of days?"

"Yes," Chad replied. "I will see this through with you."

At the end of the entrance road, Chad asked which way to turn.

"The Desert Villa Inn," Maylee said, indicating with her finger to turn right, "is away from the hustle and bustle."

They drove through downtown Barstow, which had a honky-tonk truck stop atmosphere with gas stations, inexpensive restaurants, and billboards. Palm trees lining the street seemed to be an attempt to spruce the town up, but in Chad's mind this did not succeed.

A couple of miles outside town, past modest neighborhoods of A-frame homes with only a sparse smattering of trees, they came to the inn.

Chad parked the car under a porte cochere that was covered by russet-hued terracotta tiles that matched the roof of the two-story inn. Palm trees dotted the parking lot islands, and this time they contributed a bit of class to this wide-open property that, unlike town, had plenty of elbow room, being out here in the desert sprinkled with scrubby vegetation with sand-colored hills in the distance.

"I want to pay for the room," Maylee said. They headed for the check-in desk.

Maylee's voice was soft but firm. Chad knew better than to argue. "Thank you," he said, approaching the sliding front door, which automatically opened.

Maylee stopped and took hold of Chad's wrist. "No," she said with a rise in her voice, "thank *you*, Chad." She took in the still-open doorway, nodding as if to say, *That's settled*, and walked in.

Their room was standard with a king-size bed and two cushy chairs in a sitting area.

Chad stood at the patio sliding glass door. Dusk was settling over the land. "Hungry?" he asked.

"Famished," Maylee replied. "What say I buy you dinner at the inn restaurant and we come back here and I thank you real proper-like for all you have done?"

At dinner, both passed on alcohol, Chad wanting to have all his senses for what Maylee had in store for him, and Maylee only saying to the server, "Water, please."

On the walk across the parking lot back to the room, a chill was in the air. The night sky was awash in stars. Maylee took Chad's hand, lacing her fingers with his in a firm grip. She had been quiet during dinner, not sulky quiet, but more calmly still.

Back in their bedroom, Maylee came up to Chad, wrapped an arm around his waist, and kissed him, their mouths opening, their tongues intertwined. Maylee sank her hands down Chad's shorts and pulled up his polo shirt, which he then removed. She then pulled down his zipper, the metallic *zing* triggering a wanting desire.

When they had finished undressing each other, Chad ripped back the bedcovers. Maylee lay down on her back. She had a slim, bony body with smallish breasts, generous hips, and a neat crop of dark pubic hair. She was by no means voluptuous, nor could she even be described as sexy, but it did not matter; it was her oppositeness, her poems created out of thin air, her seeing Chad for not only who he was but also who he could become that drew him to her.

Their first time together had been a delight, but this was on a different level. Maylee had an insatiable hunger, her body writhing and grinding, her grunts of pleasure stirring Chad, so that when he came, he let out an "aaahhh" groan that sounded as though a release cord had been pulled inside him.

After, they lay back, Maylee's head on his shoulder, the heat of her body like a comfortable blanket, the only sounds audible being the pulse of Maylee's heart against Chad's ribs and her deep breaths, which had settled into a slow and even rhythm.

Maylee nuzzled her face against Chad's ear and whispered, "I will always love you."

CHAPTER 13

AFTER A LATE BREAKFAST AT the inn, Maylee and Chad returned to their room.

"I'm going to call the funeral home and see when I can pick up my mother's ashes." Maylee sat on the side of the unmade bed and lifted the receiver to the phone.

Chad waited on the patio. Shortly after finishing her call, Maylee came out.

"Won't be ready until later today, and I would like to scatter her ashes tomorrow at dawn, if that's okay," she said.

"That's fine."

"If you need to get back—"

Chad cut in, "I am good, Maylee."

He stood and placed his hands on her shoulders. Their eyes met. In hers, there was uncertainty.

"What say we relax at the pool today?" Chad said.

Maylee looked out at the desert landscape, seeing a lone tumbleweed blowing across the desert. "First, I would like to take a walk."

Her tone told Chad she would like to walk by herself. "Sure," he replied, "walk and think."

After Maylee left, Chad called Monty's cell phone.

"Hello-o-o-o, old chap," Monty said with great enthusiasm.

Monty told Chad that he was parked at a rest stop in Port Angeles, Washington, waiting for Cara to return.

Chad filled Monty in on the passing of Maylee's mother, then said, "Not sure where Maylee and I stand. Ever since we left the magic of the road trip, it seems a new reality has come over her."

"She is a hard one to figure," Monty said.

"Last night she told me that she will always love me."

"What?" Monty said. "That sounds like a farewell."

"Yeah, I know, Monty. And the way she said it was as though she was moving on. Just when I thought I had met someone to spend the rest of my life with—or at least that's what I keep telling myself."

"Damn, you're getting all complicated on me."

Monty went on to say that he and Cara were having a grand time. "We complement each other," he said through a laugh. "Who knew?" He then asked if Chad and Maylee would be catching up with them.

"Seems doubtful, but I will let you know for certain in a day or two," Chad replied. "Maylee has to get busy on her rewrite, and I have decided to rededicate myself to my career."

"Now you're talking. Also," Monty said, lowering his voice an octave, "a relationship isn't always over when you think it is. Sometimes you need a break to get things straight in your life."

Late afternoon, Chad drove Maylee to the Highland Funeral Home, a rectangular single-story wood-framed structure set on a high granite-block formation with a hip roof and clapboard siding. The building, located off a two-lane road on the outskirts of town, looked like a well-preserved New England train depot situated in the middle of nowhere—an out-of-place anomaly amid this stark landscape.

Chad asked Maylee if she wanted him to come with her.

"No," she said. "I will not be long."

Ten minutes later, she returned, holding a ceramic urn. She asked Chad to open the trunk.

Back in the car, Maylee said, "It cost extra to get this all done so quick, but after tomorrow morning, I can move on with my life."

Maylee and Chad stood atop a rust-colored mesa, the sun peeking over the horizon, as the cloud-layered sky awoke to an array of morning colors.

Maylee removed the lid from the urn and took a deep breath as she extended her arm out, scattering the ashes into the wind, which brought the powdery residue back into her face. She removed her glasses and rubbed the dust off her lenses with the backs of her fingers.

"Ah, Mama," Maylee said, "you always did have to have the last word."

Chad wanted to put his arm around Maylee, but he stopped, seeing her reflective expression had a singularity to it, as though a recalculation were occurring. The rustle of wind was the only sound.

Maylee breathed in a deep breath and let out a stream of air as though a decision had been reached. "My mother and I used to drive out here and sit after"—she winced, her gaze on the hills lit purple by the first glimmers of the sun—"a drunken rage by my father."

She breathed out, her eyes rimmed with tears. "Actually," she said, grazing the knuckle of her index finger against her cheek, "it was more like an escape."

Maylee went on to say that when her father took off, she was relieved and saddened. "He was a brute, but he was the only father I had. At seven years old, I felt abandoned."

She then told about her mother's decline, as she, too, had felt abandoned. "Brought home the wrong men, who finished the job of changing her from who she had once been."

"Let's sit on that rock." Chad looked over at a flat-surfaced hunk of sandstone. After they sat, he said, "I'm a good listener."

"I didn't think it could get worse after my father left," Maylee said. "But although there wasn't the uproar of my father's drunken tirades, in its place was the heart-wrenching sadness of my mother getting dressed in her cheap tight dresses and going to some honky-tonk bar looking for Mr. Right, who was always Mr. Wrong." She ran her hand over the gritty surface of the stone. "It was hard to live through my mother's failures."

"The difficulties of childhood," Chad said, "form a resilient and competent adult."

"True," Maylee said, "but also leave a hard outer shell that can be difficult to penetrate."

"To thine own self *be* true," Chad said.

The tension had left Maylee's eyes as a calmness came over her, as if her mother's passing had broken loose something inside her. "I came out here at dawn one time on my own right before I left for college," she said. "The silence and the sky at sunrise brought things into a clear view."

Chad took Maylee's hand in his as they faced the sun lifting over the hills.

Chad and Maylee decided to head back to Los Angeles: she needed to meet with an editor assigned by the publishing house to discuss the edit of her novel, and Chad needed to check his answering machine for any acting opportunities.

On the way out of Barstow, Chad stopped at a pay phone and called Monty's mobile phone to tell him and Cara of their plans, but he got no answer. Monty was a wild card, as was Cara, who had a free-spiritedness that he thought may not equate to a long-term relationship.

But Monty was one of those people who did not overthink matters; he acted, sometimes impulsively. He had jumped back in after his divorce that not only cost him a whole lot of money but was also a big blow to his ego in that he'd lost his young wife to an even younger man. Time would tell which direction Monty and Cara's relationship would go, though they did seem a happy and uncomplicated couple.

But Chad could not describe himself and Maylee together as happy and uncomplicated. Reasonably happy, yes, but with complications that would mount when they returned to their lives in LA.

Being on the road and in each other's company continually was an intensely heightened experience for Chad. Would Maylee's gratitude for his support these last few days wear away as she entered the big new world of being a published author? What if the book was a huge hit? She would take book tours across the country, doing book signings and giving talks about her novel. Success and money have life-altering effects on people.

Chad had seen it often enough in the entertainment industry. Fellow actors who had struggled for years got a break and gained fame and big bucks, leading them to change their entire personae.

And what about Chad's promise to rededicate himself to his craft? Would he stick with it and do what needed to be done? Would he get in tip-top physical shape, check *Variety* for auditions, and contact his agent with his new plan of attack—and even join an actors' group that discussed technique and practiced scenes?

Chad was not looking forward to dealing with the diverse and dramatic personalities of an actors' group, but he had done it when he first arrived in LA, and it had helped with keeping his acting chops in shape. For Chad, acting was like a sport: if he did not practice, it affected his skill level.

At a stoplight, he glanced at Maylee.

She smiled faintly at Chad, whose heart faintly swooned, as the realization emerged that the fairy dust of the road trip had begun to fade away. What would come next was, as they say in a serial, to be continued.

CHAPTER 14

C HAD HANDED THE DIAMOND RING to Monty, who said, "I, Montague Sinclair, take thee, Cara Fitzgerald, to be my wedded wife." Monty waited for a nod from the justice of the peace, then he slid the ring on the finger of Cara, who brought to Chad's mind the song "I Love the Flower Girl."

Cara wore a light blue peasant dress, her honey-gold skin in perfect contrast to the simple yet elegant wedding gown. Her flowing blonde hair was braided in a resplendent crown of colorful flowers.

Chad, as best man, stood next to Monty, who wore a floral shirt, slacks, and sandals. Maylee served as maid of honor, standing next to Cara. The guests were seated in five rows, separated by a white aisle runner, six rattan folding chairs to a side, on a backyard hillside terrace in Malibu, overlooking the Pacific Ocean.

The view was spectacular, the water shimmering blue in the benevolent sunlight. The home was that of an older woman who was a fan of Cara's artwork. Two of her paintings hung on the walls of the ranch-style home.

As Monty kissed his new bride, applause and a few soft cheers erupted from the guests.

What a *wow* moment—Monty had actually done it. Upon returning from Barstow, Chad didn't see Monty for two weeks, as he and Cara had traveled through the Pacific Northwest up to British Columbia and back. When Chad and Monty got together over beers at a bar in Sherman Oaks, Monty told Chad, "I am going to take the plunge with Cara."

"What!" Chad had responded.

"Cannot imagine living without her." Monty motioned to the bartender for another round. He turned to Chad, his eyes possessing a steady tranquility that Chad had never seen before. "And," he added, "she feels the same way."

"Don't get mad, but did you talk about a prenuptial agreement?" Chad said, nodding thank-you to the bartender serving their beers.

"Nah," Monty said, "I just decided that she is the one, and if I screw this up, she deserves what she can get."

The reception was held on the terrace, accompanied by two waiters, a bar with two bartenders, and a DJ spinning oldies from the fifties and sixties. The guests were dressed in LA casual, mostly slacks and polo shirts for the men, with the women in silk blouses and tailored slacks, a few in long dresses.

Chad was still trying to digest the fact that in less than three months after Monty and Cara had met, they were married.

As the newlyweds made the rounds visiting with guests, Chad and Maylee stood at the wrought-iron railing along the edge of the terrace. This was the first time they had seen each other in two months. Upon returning from Barstow, Maylee only had had time to meet twice for lunch, as she had immediately begun working long hours on the rewrite of her novel with the editor. And within a couple of weeks, Chad went on location in Wyoming for a western produced by MGM; he'd just gotten back to town late last night.

Chad and Maylee had kept in touch on the phone a couple of times a week, but week by week, a distance grew between them. Maylee's words and comment came across as perfunctory. "Rewrite is going fine," she would reply in a toneless voice when Chad asked. She might mention the weather or ask about the film, but all the while Chad sensed that all she wanted to do was get back to her work.

"So," Maylee said, as she spread her fingers atop the railing, "here we are."

Chad was tempted to ask, *Where exactly are we?* But he only offered her a nod and a smile.

A waiter dressed in a white shirt and bow tie, dark vest, and matching creased pants asked if they would like a drink.

After they placed their order, Maylee said in a hushed voice, "Isn't it funny that the only person wearing a tie is the waiter? So LA."

"'LA easy' is what Monty and I came up with years ago to describe the lifestyle," Chad said, as Cara and Monty approached.

"Hello, newlyweds." Chad extended his hand to Monty, who returned a firm pumping handshake.

"Whoa," Chad said, wringing his hand in mock pain. "Someone ate their Wheaties this morning." He kissed Cara on the cheek. "You look absolutely ravishing."

"Easy there, boy," Monty said, shifting his eyes on Maylee. "You, my dear—"

"Look fabulous," Chad cut in. "As always."

"Okay," Cara said, "now that we have that determined, what does the bride have to do to get a drink around here?"

The waiter returned with Maylee and Chad's drinks on a tray. Maylee handed her wine to Cara, and Chad handed his beer to Monty. Chad then said to the waiter, "Dos más, por favor."

The waiter, who was a young Mexican, bowed and zipped off.

Cara took a generous swallow of her wine, smiled her beautiful smile, her glistening teeth in perfect contrast to her goldenness, and said, "Who would have known a Bricklin breaking down would lead to this?"

"Breaking down in Big Sur," Monty said, lifting his finger, "made all the difference."

"Really?" Chad said.

"Magic was in the air there," Monty said. "Almost poetic, don't you think, Maylee?"

The waiter came up. Chad handed Maylee her drink and then took his beer. He nodded a thank-you to the waiter, then said to Monty, "Magic, huh?"

"We were meant to be," Cara said. She grabbed Monty's hand, lifting her chin toward the other guests. "We must continue making the rounds."

"Hah," Monty said over his shoulder as they headed off. "I am already getting orders."

The departure of Cara and Monty left a void, as though the realization that their friends were married and they were not had emptied them. And for Chad, being in Maylee's presence was different, as though the intimacy of the road trip had vanished and in its place had come an unsettling distance—what they once had was no longer.

"After," Maylee said as they faced the ocean, the faint call of seagulls swooping over the water audible amid the crashing of waves on the shore, "let's go back to your place and talk." She turned her gaze on Chad, those perceptive eyes of hers making it seem as if she were reading his mind.

"I was thinking the same thing." He took Maylee's hand in his, her warm flesh against his sending a charge, like a longing, through him. "But first we will need to reacquaint ourselves." He lifted his brow as though to say, *Agreed?*

Maylee leaned forward, her face in Chad's ear and said softly: "Reacquaint is quaint, / Though no poet would say, / But it is the essence of what will be / In the lives of Chad and Maylee."

Chad's house was on a cul-de-sac off Mulholland Drive, with a view of the Santa Monica Valley. He had purchased the house, which needed plenty of work, after he made a good chunk of money in 1977 doing a string of commercials for Schlitz beer. The commercials were hokey. In one he played a football player: "Take away my Schlitz, take away my gusto. I am going to send you out for a long pass and you will come back incomplete."

He almost didn't take the job, worried about the stigma of becoming known as a commercial actor, but his agent talked him into it by mentioning actors and actresses who had gotten their big breaks from doing a commercial.

Chad didn't get his breakthrough part from the ads, but they bought him the house, which was in a great location near the studios in the valley and not that far from a string of beach towns teeming with young lovelies.

And the price had made it a steal, so he spent all his spare time fixing up his "little ranch in the hills," having gained his carpentry skills from building sets during summer stock. He replaced cabinets and appliances in the kitchen, rehabbed the two bathrooms, and tore out the ragged wall-to-wall carpets, discovering teak floors, which he refinished.

He then tackled the jungle of weeds and vines that had taken over the quarter-acre property. He planted ground cover and a few rock gardens with low-maintenance shrubs.

His last and most difficult task was tearing up the decrepit flagstone terrace, with a failing stone wall perimeter, and then rebuilding the wall and laying a new patio.

After two years, his work finished, he had a fine house that a realtor neighbor told him had increased in value nearly double what he had paid.

After their *reacquaintance*, Chad and Maylee went to his terrace, the sun setting over the valley. Chad enjoyed this time of day in this location, the valley aglitter in a swath of light from the streetlamps and homes, the sky streaked in shades of violet.

They sat next to each other, the chirps of crickets and a hoot of a barn owl the only sounds.

"How is *Desert Girl* coming along?" Chad asked.

"Finished, and the publisher is fast-tracking publication."

"Reel-lee," Chad said, stretching out the word *really*. "What is the plan?"

Maylee's left hand gripped the edge of the armrest of her wicker chair. She took a long breath. "I have always enjoyed this space, the view ... the company ..."

Chad sensed what was coming. She had said "have always," the present perfect tense, denoting an action just completed—in the same vein as "I will always love you."

"The plan," Maylee said, "is a two-month book tour across the country after the book comes out. The publishing house thinks I have written a best seller."

"That's great," Chad said, though his tone did not match his words.

"Yes, it's what I have wanted since I started writing," Maylee said. "But I am not sure where all this leaves us."

"When is the book coming out?"

"In six weeks." Maylee folded her hands on her lap, her expression that of a person who had made a decision, her lips pursed, her jaw set. "I think," she said, "we both need to concentrate on our careers."

"You have your book tour coming up." Chad felt a queasy uncertainty stirring inside him—a moment of truth.

They turned toward each other, Maylee's face like a shadow.

"Maybe later," she said. "We can reconnect after—"

"The dust settles." Chad reached for Maylee's hand, their fingers interlacing. "And we both find that elusive creature called success."

There was nary a hoot or audible chirp, the valley looking like a glowing strip wedged within the shadowy darkness as the sun had sunk below the horizon.

Over the course of the ensuing weeks, Chad had considered trying to convince Maylee out of their separation, but he didn't want to beg, especially when she was so adamant. And also, he thought she might be on to something: they both did need to devote themselves to their careers for the time being.

Although heartbroken, Chad instinctively knew he could not allow himself to sink into a deep ravine of depression. Over the years, he had witnessed the devastation of rejection his colleagues experienced from failures either in their careers or their love lives. Some never recovered and were never heard of or seen again. Others partially recovered but, in the process, had lost an edge, a confidence, that had left them shells of their former selves on and off the set.

So, to combat his heartbreak, Chad sank every bit of himself into reviving his career. He joined an actors' group that met twice a week to rehearse scenes,

continued his exercise regimen of running the hills of his neighborhood and going to the gym, and auditioning for and winning the role of Theodore "Hickey" Hickman in *The Iceman Cometh* at the Pacific Resident Theater in Venice.

The rehearsals were six days a week and were long and intense, but they honed Chad's thespian skills. He knew not only his own lines inside and out but also every other character's lines.

The play is set in a New York bar teeming with alcoholics who are anticipating the semiannual visit of Hickey, a charismatic traveling salesman who is the life of the party.

Chad got into Hickey's complex character with every ounce of his being. He dreamt he was Hickey, felt his anguish, his delusions, and the overall sense of a failed life.

CHAPTER 15

I T HAD BEEN OVER A year since Chad had last seen Maylee, their last night together having been spent at his place after Cara and Monty's wedding. He had oftentimes considered calling her, and kept waiting for a call from her that never came. It hurt like nothing he had ever experienced. Not so much the rejection—though that stung—but what she had brought to his life, a life that he did not want to live 'til death all alone. Rather—much more than rather—he wanted someone to talk with who would share not only her day but also her dreams.

Immersing himself in work and studying his craft had helped ease the agony. Chad had taken the pain of his being separated from Maylee and harnessed it into an effort to work and study his way out of it, though it had been a painful withdrawal. The former wound was now a healed scar, but he still thought of the relationship with a what-if.

But all the pain and effort had paid off, as Chad had gotten the lead in a major film.

"Chad, I need you show more desperation. More!"

Chad nodded to the young director, Quincy Tarenton, an up-and-comer who had received an Oscar nomination for his screenplay *No Tell Motel*, a production that he also had directed. "Got it, Quincy."

Quincy had selected Chad for the lead in *Sundown at El Diablo* after seeing his performance in *The Iceman Cometh*.

It was late morning of the first day of filming, which had moved to the saloon at the Paramount Ranch in Agoura Hills, a famous and often-used site for westerns. Chad was playing Billy Hargrove, a roving ranch hand in the late 1890s who was past his prime, his carousing ways having caught up with him.

At sunrise they had already filmed the opening scene, where Billy is robbed and beaten and left for dead in a canyon. Bloody and bruised, Billy walks for two days in the blistering sun before straggling into town.

"Quiet on the set," Quincy said with a lift of his hand. "Action."

The saloon doors flapped open. Chad stepped inside the saloon, wobbling as he made his way to the bar.

BILLY, *in a halting, scratchy voice.* I need water. (*Shoots a hollowed-eye look at the bartender before keeling over.*)

"Cut," Quincy ordered. "Yes, Chad, yes. That is desperation."

The remainder of the morning, they filmed Billy's recovery in the room of a barmaid, who tenderly tended to him in silent clips showing the progression of time. After which Quincy said, "Let's break for lunch."

This was all new to Chad, the lead in a major film, with Quincy Tarenton directing no less. He had his own trailer and his own actor's chair with his name scrolled across the back. Getting to this point over the last fifteen months had been a grind and a challenge, but his dedication had paid off.

After lunch with a few crew members, Chad had some time to kill while the set was prepped for the next scene, so he decided to return to his trailer to study the script.

The next scene was with his costar Alexa Vandross, who played the barmaid, Lola Langston, his romantic interest in the movie. Alexa was in her early forties. Having become a star at twenty-one, she had fallen on lean times as many actresses her age had experienced. Costarring in this film must have been a welcome assignment.

Opening the door to his trailer, Chad discovered Alexa sitting on a sofa, script in hand. "Hope you don't mind," she said, peering over her reading glasses. "I thought we could go over the upcoming scene."

"Oh," Chad said, stepping up and inside, eyeing Alexa warily in her saloon girl costume, a period piece, a brightly colored ruffled dress, the bodice cut low over her generous bosom, her well-sculpted arms and shoulders bare.

Alexa removed her glasses and patted the sofa. "Sit, Billy Hargrove. If we're going to be lovers, we need to *be* lovers."

Chad's one and only fling on a set was with the beguiling bombshell Monica Healey all those years ago on the *Gunsmoke* set. That did not end well. Not that he was now worried about falling for Alexa. And there was no woman in his life presently, though he still thought daily about Maylee, wondering if she had moved on to another man, maybe a fellow author? Did she still think about Chad? It hurt him to think about her.

So, he was a free agent, and *damn*, Alexa was a good-looking, sexy woman with brunette hair and a welcoming glint in her eyes.

Chad sat down next to Alexa. "I am all yours, Lola."

After a thoroughly enjoyable romp in the sack with the uninhibited Alexa, the two headed back to the set.

When they entered the saloon, they found Quincy huddled with the assistant director and a couple of members of the crew, with grips scurrying about setting up drinks on the bar, while techs arranged open-face lighting fixtures.

Everything stopped as the male and female leads arrived. In that quicksilver moment, a question seemed to have settled over the crew: *Are they an item—already?*

Quincy spent nearly an hour getting the bar scene just so. He had tables moved and discussed the angle shots with his cameramen. Finally he said, "All right, everyone, take your places."

The actors went to their marks, the cameraman got set, the crew moved behind the camera, and Quincy shouted, "Action!"

RAYMOND COSGROVE. Billy Hargrove, you lowlife varmint, you done barked up the wrong tree, pard.

(*Billy cradles his shot of whiskey, lifts it, and throws down his drink.*)

BILLY. I ain't your pard, Cosgrove. (*Glances at Lola, who is standing at his side, and slides a look down the bar at the beefy and unshaven galoot.*)

COSGROVE. Lola! (*Pounds his big fist on the bar.*) Come over here.

LOLA, *in a silky-smooth singsong voice.* Raymond Cosgrove, I don't belong to you.

(*Billy throws a look at Lola and then turns and faces Cosgrove.*)

BILLY. I am unarmed, so I figure you have two choices. (*Narrows his gaze at Cosgrove, who stands there reeking belligerence.*) You can shoot me dead and hang, or we can head out to the street. (*Cocks his head, squinting a dare at Cosgrove.*) And get yourself an ass-whupping. (*Makes a face.*) What's it gonna be?

"Cut," Quincy said. "You nailed it, Chad—all of you did." He came down from his director's chair. "All right, let's move out to the street."

And so it went. The days were long, with much standing around, as Quincy had to get everything positioned just so. During lunch breaks, Chad and Alexa headed for Chad's trailer together. It was known on the set that they were *involved*. But it wasn't as though one was married and cheating on an unknowing spouse.

They didn't see each other away from the set, having their sexual therapy, as Alexa called it, during breaks in filming.

Alexa was uninhibited in regard to lovemaking, her tongue and lips exploring various regions of Chad's body. After they'd have intercourse, they'd talk mostly about the script or some movie industry tidbit. They had achieved a tacit understanding, through Alexa's nonchalance—a no-big-deal attitude—toward their lovemaking that this was a temporary arrangement. They both knew that once the filming was completed, she would move on to another set and another temporary lover.

Alexa reminded Chad of a roguish man in her approach to the opposite sex: enjoy the pleasure of each other's bodies and move on to the next—a female version of him and Monty back in the day.

Lola had been married twice, the first time in her early twenties to a young man who was her equal in stardom. But that young man fell in love on the set of a big action film with his costar and went on to divorce Alexa, who, according to the tabloids, was devastated.

On the rebound, she married an older man, who was a successful entertainment attorney, but this time it was she who had left him.

So, the Alexa today, at age forty-two, was probably not the same person that she was twenty years ago. With the scar tissue from her marriages there had come a permanent alteration: she was a reasonably happy individual, but she had no hint of commitment in regard to Chad.

Still, she was definitely committed to her craft. She was a talented actress with a keen eye in regard to the performance of her fellow actors.

During breaks, Alexa and Chad would analyze the upcoming scenes and discuss how to play them. "You need to look at me as though I am the reincarnation of the first girl you fell for, the first girl you kissed." Alexa let her infatuated gaze settle on Chad. "Like this." She leaned forward, kissing him on the lips, her hand cupping the back of his neck. "Sell out, Chad, with everything you have."

The movie progressed on schedule, with Billy taking a job as a hand at the biggest ranch in the area and working his way up to foreman after exhibiting great skills as a cowhand, including breaking an unbreakable stallion and saving the life of the ranch owner's son. Then came the engagement to Lola, and all seemed so fine in the life of Billy Hargrove, who was still leery. "I do not trust happiness," he had told a hand on the ranch in a moment of reflection. It was a line said by Maylee in Chad's dream the first night they had met, and Chad had convinced Quincy to insert it in the script.

And then it all came true when, two days before the wedding, Lola ran off with a handsome gambler, leaving a brokenhearted Billy to go on a bender, lose his job, and accidentally kill a ranch hand in a drunken brawl at the saloon.

Billy rode off, but he lost his horse when they had a fall trying to climb a steep hillside.

Under a searing sun, Billy walked all day, looking over his shoulder for a posse, until he ended up in a desolate canyon. Delirious and out of water, Billy confronted a red-streaked horizon, the glowing red sun sinking below the hills.

BILLY, *mumbling through parched lips.* Should have known that happiness is an illusion.

Fade out.

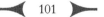

The wrap party was held a week later at Quincy's home in Beverly Hills. It was an old mansion that he had sunk a small fortune into rehabbing, situated on a half-acre two blocks from downtown.

A security guard at the gate greeted Chad with a jaunty salute. "Mr. Carson," he said in a respectful tone, "welcome." He opened the iron gate and waved Chad through.

"How about that, getting the celebrity treatment," Chad said aloud as he drove up to the circular drive in front of the house, a gaudy castle-like affair of balustrades, arches, and an ornamental parapet, all intertwined in intricate stonework.

A young man in a short-sleeved white shirt and bow tie waved Chad to the front of the house. He leaned over to the open driver's-side window and said, "Parking attendant at your service, Mr. Carson." He then opened the door.

Chad had been recognized in public before, but few people knew his name. Two in a row was more than a coincidence. He got out of the car and said, "How did you know my name?"

"Mr. Tarenton provided the staff pictures with the names of every member of the cast and even tested us."

Chad handed him the keys and said, "I bet you didn't have to remember Alexa Vandross."

A butler, dressed in a black waistcoat and vest, holding a vest watch on a chain, opened the door before Chad could knock. "Sir," the servant said in a haughty British accent, "this way if you please." He turned his wrist over in a slow theatrical manner—like a caricature of a stereotypical butler in movies from the forties—gesturing with his hand to the long hallway, and then up three steps to an open area with high ceilings.

At the top of the steps, Chad saw Quincy giving instructions to three waitresses dressed in black slacks and white dress shirts with red bow ties. They were all beautiful and more than likely aspiring actresses.

Around the perimeter of the open space, bars were set up in the two back corners. On a raised dais along a side wall, a band—dressed in tuxedos—with a piano, two horns, and drums was warming up with spurts of music.

Only a few guests had arrived. All appeared to be crew members, dressed in the typical LA casual, polo shirts and shorts or slacks.

Quincy spotted Chad and came over to him, his hand extended. "Welcome, Chad, my good man," he said in an exuberant voice, a broad smile splitting his lean, angular face. Quincy looked the part of new-wave auteur: purple silk scarf around the neck, beige camel hair sports coat, floral shirt, creased blue jeans, and tan and white wing tip shoes.

Quincy opened his mouth, then seemed to think better of speaking. He peered over Chad's shoulder, his brow furrowed. "Ah, someone here you need to meet, Chad." He tapped Chad on the shoulder and said, "Later."

He stepped around and past Chad and extended his hand to a bald-headed man in his early sixties, a towering figure who stood a good six foot four in height.

"William," Quincy said, "so glad you could make it."

William, dressed in a pinstripe suit, starched white shirt, and dark blue tie, appeared out of place amongst the LA casual, possibly an East Coast elite businessman, who gave the impression of power, someone with clout.

Soon, the room was abuzz with nearly everyone from the cast and crew present, well over one hundred people: cameraman, grips, gaffers, boom operators, production designers, and so forth.

Then as if on cue, Alexa arrived, her curvaceous body straining at the fabric of a low-cut red dress, her ample breasts nearly spilling out. She looked stunning. Alongside her was a rumpled fellow in his midfifties wearing an untucked long-sleeved beige silk shirt, Bermuda shorts, penny loafers with no socks, and a blue Dodgers ball cap atop his head, with acres of curly hair spilling out around the edges. He looked familiar to Chad, but Chad could not place him. Possibly some big shot in the industry.

Quincy darted over and greeted Alexa with a kiss on both cheeks. He shook hands with her companion. "Matthew, so good to see you," Quincy said in a ringing voice, giving a pat on Matthew's shoulder.

The two men conversed in muffled voices for a minute before Quincy was off greeting other arriving guests.

The band had started playing lively jazz songs from the forties. The party mushroomed into a spirited gathering, the crew members laughing and recounting the hard work they had put into the making of the film.

Over at the bar, Matthew chatted with William, who stood ramrod straight, martini in hand. They seemed an odd pair, the towering, distinguished-looking William in his expensive suit, and the frumpy Matthew in his ball cap and frat boy outfit, a middle-aged man in search of his youth.

Chad caught Alexa's eye. As he approached, her mouth twisted in a "Been there, done that" parting of the lips.

"Hello, Chad," she said.

Matthew appeared. "Here we are," he said, handing Alexa a glass of red wine. He turned to Chad. "Hi there. Matthew Levine here."

Oh yes, Chad thought, *the famous producer.* "Nice to meet you, Matthew.

Chad—"

"Chad Carson," Matthew cut in. "Quincy showed me some dailies of your performance in *Sundown at El Diablo*—"

Matthew's attention was diverted as Quincy and William appeared and introductions were made. William was the managing editor for Random House.

"Let me get right to the point," William said. "Random House has the movie rights to a best seller that is being fast-tracked into production." He leveled his gaze on Chad. "Matthew thinks you would be perfect for one of the major roles."

"We have already signed Alexa, and Quincy to direct," Matthew said. All eyes were on Chad.

"Let me guess, the best seller you are referring to," Chad said as he felt the hair on the back of his neck rise, "is called *Desert Girl*."

CHAPTER 16

C HAD HAD BEEN AWARE THAT *Desert Girl* was a best seller, but he'd never gotten around to reading it. Why that was, he was not sure, other than a gut feeling to wait.

Two weeks before reporting for the first day of filming in Barstow, Chad read the screenplay, written by Quincy. The mother's character would be played by Alexa. It was a compelling read, telling the story of Macy Leeward's journey from Barstow to Berkeley. It went along with what Maylee had told Chad, but with a huge part missing: Macy had been raped at age fourteen by her mother's boyfriend, the character Chad would be playing. Chad recalled what Maylee had told him: "I have not been with a lot of men. First time, I'd rather not talk about." No wonder. And no wonder she had not been with a lot of men.

Quincy had told Chad that Maylee would be on the set as a technical adviser, but Chad had yet to hear from her.

The lead characters and the higher-ups would be staying at the Desert Villa Inn, where Chad and Maylee had previously stayed.

The day before filming, Chad checked into the inn and was given a note by the clerk. It was from Quincy, who asked him to report to a conference room at six.

Chad's room was next door to the one he and Maylee had stayed in. He went out on the patio, the sandy-brown desert stretching out to the hills in the distance. This vast wasteland had an intriguing loneliness, this land where he would be working for the next two months, this land where worlds were colliding.

He figured that Maylee must know that he had a role in the movie, must know that she would see him in the inn and on the set. And what about Alexa?

Two sharp knocks diverted Chad's attention.

He opened the door. "Alexa."

There she stood, wearing a long-sleeved T-shirt, short-shorts, and sandals, looking beautifully insouciant. "Can we talk a minute?"

Chad motioned her inside and out to the patio. He motioned with his hand to a chair. They sat.

"Nice view, huh?" Alexa said, her narrowing gaze steady on the landscape. "We won't be fucking each other this time around." She threw a look at Chad: *Understand?*

"Strictly professional," Chad said, breathing an inward sigh of relief.

"Not that it wasn't fine and dandy last time around." Alexa crossed her legs, accentuating her well-toned thigh muscles. "But I am with Matthew, who has big plans for my career."

Alexa stood and brought the tortoiseshell sunglasses atop her head down over her eyes. "I will see you at the meeting at six, Mr. Chad Carson. Or should I say Edgar Smith?"

"Good enough, Ms. Alexa Vandross. Or should I say Eunice Leeward?"

Alexa flashed her Hollywood starlet smile and nodded. "Glad we are on the same page."

Chad arrived a few minutes early at the meeting room and found Quincy, Alexa, and Matthew sitting at a large round table in high-back chairs.

"There he is," Quincy said, motioning with his hand for Chad to sit. "I ordered this roundtable, Chad, so that we all have eye contact without feeling crowded."

"Works for me," Chad said, extending his hand to Matthew. "Mr. Producer, good to see you." He nodded a hello to Alexa, who returned the favor.

The door opened and Maylee entered.

Oh my God. It had been well over a year since Chad had last seen Maylee, and what a difference: she wore no glasses, so now her big brown eyes and perfectly flared eyebrows, which he had not noticed before, were accentuated. He remembered Eunice's comment at the nursing home: "She would look much prettier if she would get rid of those god-awful glasses, don't you think?"

Maylee's hair was shorter, in a pageboy, framing her face, which now looked fuller and not as sharp, giving her an appealing look highlighted by her high cheekbones. This was no plain Jane, but an attractive woman who projected the vibe of one who had found her true calling as a successful author.

"Aha," Quincy said, "the author has entered the building."

There was a seat open between Chad and Quincy and one between Quincy and Alexa. Maylee gave a noncommittal glance in Chad's direction before sitting next to Alexa and across the table from Chad. She lifted her brow in his direction: *Hello there, stranger.*

"Chad and Alexa, I believe you are the only ones who have not met the author," Quincy said. "May I introduce you to Maylee Lee or her singular nom de plume, Maylee. Maylee—Chad Carson and Alexa Vandross."

Chad stretched his hand out across the table. Maylee shook it, the feel of her hand in his bringing back a whirlwind of memories, a whirlwind of longing.

Alexa extend her hand to Maylee. "I loved your novel," she said with meaning.

Chad was not sure if she was sincere or if it was the actress scoring points with the author.

As Quincy went over the schedule and his interpretation of the characters, Chad and Maylee exchanged fleeting glances, an inquisitive slant of the eyes across the table, while facing Quincy.

"As you all know," Quincy said, squinting and grimacing, "Carey Brewer was cast to play Macy Leeward." He sighed and scratched in two upward strokes beneath his chin. "But she has bowed out." He looked around the table as though expecting a question. "So we held auditions here in Barstow and have hired a local girl named Angie Winter."

Maylee shot a look at Chad. *Is he serious?* She said to Quincy, "Carey Brewer was perfect for the part. She has the ability to portray vulnerability and yet strength, which is critical."

"True," Matthew said, tapping his knuckles on the table. He got up and went to a wall phone, which he picked up and dialed, soon asking for room 121. "Angie, we are ready for you."

"Angie is going to come down and do a scene with Alexa and then Chad." Quincy folded his hands on the table, his eyes on Maylee, who appeared noncommittal. He reached into a satchel on the floor, removed two copies of the screenplay, and handed one to each of the actors. "Alexa, I'd like you to turn to the top of page five. Chad, your scene is after the break on page seventy-two."

The door opened and a teenage girl appeared, wearing a hoodie and jeans. She had dark brown hair and matching eyes, the haunting eyes of an old soul. "Hello," she said in a soft yet confident voice.

After introductions were made, Angie and Alexa were up first. The scene was the morning after a terrible row between Macy's parents, the father having left for good.

"Things will get better now that he has left, Macy," Alexa said with a slight twang to her voice so that *things* was pronounced "thangs."

"Oh, Mama," Angie said with an ache in her voice, a raw look of abandonment in her eyes, which were now probing Alexa's face.

"What say today we take a drive to our special place?" Alexa said with a lift of her brow in conjunction with a bright smile that failed to hide the hurt in her eyes.

These two actresses were using facial expressions to show their true feelings; it was as though they were tuned to the same wavelength.

"Won't Daddy come back for Christmas?" Angie tilted her head to the side, her mouth slightly askew. There was a desperateness written across her face.

They stared at each other for a beat as Alexa's eyes said, *No.*

"On the way back, we can stop for lunch at the Carriage House." Alexa placed her hand on her Angie's cheek.

Angie drew her lips in, top over bottom, hollowing her cheeks, before exhaling. "That'll be fine, Mama."

The next scene had Chad, as Edgar, showing up at the trailer with only Macy there.

"Your mother here, girl?" Chad demanded as he scanned the space like a soldier on patrol.

"She won't be back from the diner until after the dinner rush," Angie said. She was sitting at the table, the others standing off, intently watching the scene.

"Well now," Chad said, stepping toward the table, "I reckon it's just you and me, girl."

Angie's expression dropped, her mouth agape, a tinge of fear in her eyes.

"How old you be, girl?" Chad demanded. He placed his hand on the table, a lean and hungry look coming over him.

"Four ... teen," Angie said cautiously, dropping her gaze to the floor. She looked up as if an idea had come to her. "Can I fix you something to eat before Mama comes home?"

"Ain't hungry ... for food, that is," Chad said. He clutched Angie's wrist.

"Please," Angie said in the most sorrowful of voices.

"That's good," Quincy said. He turned to Maylee and lifted his brow as though to ask, *Well?*

"Angie," Maylee said with conviction, "I am honored to have you play Macy."

After the meeting, Chad and Maylee were the last to leave, trailing the others.

"Congratulations on the book," Chad said as they came to a halt in the lobby, where there were a few people milling about. Being back in her presence brought on a light-headed longing, as her absence from his life had left a void that roared to the forefront like a runaway train. He wanted to scream, *I missed you!*

"Good to see you again, Chad."

Though Maylee's words were spoken in a mild and friendly tone, her eyes were speaking volumes with a look of one refinding a lost treasure. "And congratulations on your performance in *Sundown at El Diablo*. Matthew thinks you will be nominated for an Oscar."

Chad had heard a few such rumors about the Oscar but had not taken them very seriously. But if Matthew said it, well, there just might be something there. "It seems ..." He paused, searching for the right word.

"The dust has settled," Maylee said. There was now an excitement in her eyes, like a promise of things to come—new things.

"Shall we sit?" Chad said, looking to a pair of wingback chairs in the corner of the lobby.

"You look great," Chad said. They sat facing each other. "No glasses. Contacts?"

"Yes," Maylee said. "My agent suggested it."

"Question."

"Yes?"

"Why did you break off with me?" Chad thought he knew the reason, but he needed to hear her say it.

"I knew ... no, I sensed," Maylee said as she placed her hand over her heart, "that I needed to go off on my own and absorb everything that had happened and was about to happen—my mother passing, the book, the hoopla of the upcoming publicity tour. As much as not having you in my life made me feel so terribly empty, at that moment it was my only choice. I feared if we stayed together at that point that it would have irrevocably ended."

"It hurt so bad," Chad said. "But the pain of you not in my life pushed me to work and study my craft like never before."

"Countless times I was tempted to call you, but ..." Maylee's eyes lifted as a *that's the way it was* look came over her. "But we both had things to sort out before *we* could *be*."

"I felt that there was a chance of us getting back together, but after a while ..." Chad shrugged as if to say, *Not sure*.

"I knew there was a risk of losing you to someone else who might enter your life, but it was a chance I had to take."

"I think you knew deep down that that wouldn't happen."

"Consciously, no." Maylee lifted her hand to the back of her head and said, "Subconsciously, quite possibly."

A burst of warm laughter turned their attention to a cluster of folks at the front desk who were hugging and chattering in the way of people who are seeing each other after a time apart—a family reunion possibly, three generations, from little ones up to what looked like grandparents, aunts, and uncles.

Maylee and Chad shifted their attention back to each other. Maylee took him in with those eyes of hers transmitting a look of eternal reassurance—*Now and only now were we meant to be*.

They sat there absorbing each other's look, Chad flushed with the comfort and sense of well-being that came from being in her presence.

He lifted his hands, indicating a new topic. "Did you have anything to do with me getting the part of Edgar Smith?"

Maylee sat back, her elbows on the armrests, her hands folded. "No," she replied, "but when they mentioned you as their top choice, I thought how things were coming full circle."

"Edgar Smith," Chad said as he leaned forward, hands on knees, "is going to take my full concentration." He studied her face to see her reaction.

"Do you remember the Ansel Adams photograph at the art museum in Monterey, *Lodgepole Pines*?"

"Yes," Chad said as he eased back in his chair. "Your first poem, but not in its entirety."

"That's where a photographic memory comes in handy," Maylee said. "Sitting on the banks of the Merced River, / Absorbed in the darkness and light, / I imagine my future in peaceful flight. / But if I soared high above the shadow and glow, / Will I still maintain my eternal flow? / Only one way to know, but do go slow, / For the unknown is a mystery, or so caws the crow."

Maylee said, "The penultimate line is the key."

"So we keep it strictly professional during filming," Chad said.

"Agreed."

"When Monty and I did the Butch and Sundance scene for you and Cara, that was the moment I realized I needed to rededicate myself to my craft."

"You were so good," Maylee said.

"I wanted to impress you. In attempting to do so, it triggered a reboot in not just my career but also"—Chad tapped his fist over his heart—"in me," he said, a swell of emotion swirling in his throat. "You made me want to become a better person."

"And you," Maylee said in a particular tone of discovery, "were a godsend at a critical point in my life." She lifted her brow and added, "Not sure where I would be if ..." She shrugged, her eyes saying, *Thank you.*

"So, there we have it," Chad said. "Another detour that holds promise for better days."

Maylee's eyes brightened as though she'd just discovered an old friend returning from a wayward journey.

"Incoming?" Chad asked.

Maylee wagged a finger at Chad and began: "A shift in the paradigm / From when last they met, / As they advance wittingly / In pursuit of their dreams / To live the life imagined. / Having met with success, / Unexpected in common hours, / Fate intervenes as a / New beginning arrives, / In the land of moviemaking dreams."

CHAPTER 17

C HAD HAD THROWN HIMSELF INTO the character Edgar Smith, a dangerous roughneck who could be charming one moment and turn scary-bad the next.

Two weeks into filming, he had already completed scenes that showed Edgar released from prison and being hired as a laborer repairing railroad lines. Today they were filming his first time meeting Eunice at the diner. The set was on a ranch not far from the inn. Other scenes would be filmed in and around Barstow.

To make Chad more believable as Edgar, his hair had been cut military short and he'd been given a fake scar slashing his cheek. He'd also grown a goatee, which when encased by a crooked smile, contributed to the sinister transformation. But even more than that, when in character, Chad took on Edgar's persona with a snarly curl of the lip, a narrowing of the eyes, and a swaggering badass strut. Inside and out, he was Edgar Smith. And Angie and Alexa were knocking it out of the park with their performances.

This movie had great potential, but Chad had been in the business long enough to know that nothing was guaranteed. He had been in films that he was certain would be a hit but then turned out to be failures, and vice versa.

Quincy, having purchased a trailer and a local diner that had gone out of business, had moved both to the set. He had put his own personal touches on the diner to give it an early seventies style, with a tabletop jukebox at each table, a black and white checkered linoleum floor, and a gaudy neon sign atop the structure advertising the name, Desperado Diner.

On Monday morning of the third week of filming, Chad's scene was up first. His character would be driving a battered pickup into the diner parking lot:

Edgar gets out of the truck, grimacing his badass persona in full force.

He enters the diner, with extras, mostly construction types in work shirts and denim, sitting in booths and at the front counter. Edgar sits on a stool at the front counter and spots Eunice pouring coffee, her back to him, her curvy body fitting nice and tight into her waitress uniform.

Edgar's countenance changes: his brow lifts, his eyes open agreeably wide, and a toothy smile emerges from beneath the cover of his facial hair.

As Eunice turns, their eyes lock for a moment.

EDGAR, *in a voice just as nice as could be.* I'll take a coffee black, when you get a chance.

Eunice looks at Edgar as though she is liking what she is seeing.
"Cut," Quincy said. He walked up to the counter. "Chad, you are Edgar Smith. Perfect."

"Let's keep it rolling," Chad said, trying to stay in character, not wanting to lose his edge.

"Hold on, Chad," Quincy said. "Alexa, I want you to show hesitant interest in Edgar. Appear attracted but unsure of this stranger."

"Like my fellow thespian said," Alexa said, cocking her hand on hip, "let's keep it rolling, Mr. Director."

By the end of the scene, Edgar had gotten Eunice's phone number and a tentative date for Saturday night.

"Next scene is at the trailer," Quincy said to the camera crew and techs, who began the process of moving equipment. Quincy then asked Chad if they could have a word.

They went outside and off to the side as the crew began moving lights, cameras, light reflectors, and such to the trailer. "I got a heads-up on the Academy Award nominations," Quincy said. He hollered to a team of grips moving tall light fixtures, telling them where he wanted the fixtures located in the trailer. Then, turning his attention back to

Chad, he shook his head and made a clicking sound with his tongue, like tumblers on a safe. "*Sundown at El Diablo* received two nominations."

Chad could tell by Quincy's tamped-down manner that he hadn't been nominated. "Let me guess," Chad said. "Screenplay is one of them."

"Yes," Quincy said, "and Alexa for leading actress."

"Really," Chad said, realizing how big this would be for Alexa's career.

"You should have gotten the nod," Quincy said as he watched the crew moving the camera. "Hey, Eddie," he said to a crew member, "make sure we have Zeiss lenses for this shot."

"I'm glad for you and Alexa," Chad said.

"Tell you what," Quincy said. "You keep your performance up in this film, and you will not only get a nomination but also win an Oscar."

The remainder of the week was spent filming Edgar's confirmation phone call securing the date with Eunice, "dinner and dancing the night away," then at the trailer, Edgar picking up Eunice for their date and meeting Macy, all the while keeping his demeanor of a wolf in sheep's clothing. He maintained an inner meanness but also an outward glow as he played a bad man acting like a good man.

Saturday night of the third week on location, Chad had dinner brought to his room at the inn. He ate with gusto, being hungry and in a hurry, as he wanted to go over his lines for tomorrow's scenes, which would be filmed at a local restaurant and bar.

He grabbed a beer from the minifridge and went out to the patio, screenplay in hand. A few minutes into studying his lines, he got up to answer a knock at the door.

"Maylee."

"Have a minute?"

On the way to the patio, Chad asked if she would like a beer. "No, wine," he said.

"I'm good," Maylee said as they sat. She took in the dusk settling over the desert, the horizon streaked in a medley of colors. "This sure brings back memories."

As they had agreed upon, Chad and Maylee had kept their relationship on hold. They would act cordial on the set or if they saw each other at the inn, but that was it. As far as anyone knew, they were actor and author with no other connection.

"I have not suggested much to Quincy in regard to Macy's character." Maylee leaned forward in her chair, her hands on her knees. "But there's a scene later in the movie that veers off from the book that I wanted to run by you before I proceed."

Chad took a long swallow of his beer, finishing it. "Hold that thought." He got up and returned with another beer. "Yes, Maylee," he said, "what is it?"

Maylee did not want the scene with the actual rape to appear in the film. She told Chad that it would be more powerful, as it was in the book, to show Macy's clothes being ripped off, along with the fear in her face. And then after, as the script said, the viewers would see "Angie lying on the sofa naked in the fetal position, whimpering."

"I don't even remember most of it," Maylee added. "But what I will never forget, for as long as I live, was the aftermath, lying alone and violated. Negative space is a powerful tool in writing fiction and, I believe, in film. Leave the rape to the audience's imagination."

"You know, Maylee," Chad said as he ran his finger around the rim of his beer can, "I think you are on to something." He took a swallow of his beer and said, "But I suspect it will be hard to convince Quincy to alter his screenplay. I will follow up with Quincy after you."

CHAPTER 18

FOR THE NEXT MONTH, CHAD stayed focused on staying in character. After work on the set, he would head back to the inn, eat dinner in his room, and then go over the script, working out in his mind every minute detail in regard to how he should play the upcoming scene. He practiced in the mirror facial expressions and voice. He had developed a raspy growl that Quincy said was devastatingly effective. Body language and other character traits were also among the things he spent his time honing.

He intentionally did not socialize off the set, wanting to keep his distance from the cast, not wanting to stray too far from Edgar's mindset. He especially kept his distance from Angie, who was actually seventeen playing a fourteen-year-old girl, a girl whom, in tomorrow's filming, the script had his character raping.

As Chad had thought, Quincy had turned down Maylee's request to omit the rape scene, telling her the audience would feel cheated, but Chad had put off talking with Quincy about his being in agreement with Maylee because he did not want to interrupt his actor's rhythm.

But today he was off, with Quincy doing location shots, so it was now or never.

Quincy was an early riser. Chad often found him in the inn's fitness room before the sun rose.

Chad made a cup of tea and went out to the patio, the desert a shadowy space, the hills a dark outline, the sky aglitter in stars. He remembered Maylee mentioning the power of negative space, a gap in a story whose aftermath would lead the reader, or in this case the audience, to register, through the actor's emotions, the full force of the rape more powerfully than if witnessing the act.

And Angie had the acting chops to pull this off. The young woman was a nuanced and talented actress who emoted with her facial expressions and movements with such distinct clarity.

Chad had an idea. He finished his tea and changed into his workout gear.

The fitness room was empty. Chad checked the wall clock—five thirty. This facility was better than most found at a hotel. Besides a plateglass window with a view of the desert, there were four Lifecycle bikes, various resistance-training apparatuses, and two treadmills.

Quincy was departing the inn at eight for the location shots, so he still had time to show up. Meanwhile, Chad decided to ride a Lifecycle.

Besides providing a good workout, the Lifecycle provided time to think, a form of multitasking. Chad set the resistance to nine and began pedaling slowly, working his way up to a steady pace for four minutes, followed by a vigorous minute. This was his routine for forty-five minutes, including a five-minute cooldown at the end.

By ten minutes to the six, Chad was considering going to Quincy's room, when the director showed up dressed in purple shorts, a tie-dyed T-shirt, and orange sneakers. Quincy did nothing conventionally, from his dress to the manner in which he directed a movie, where he treated everyone equal, from grips to stars.

"Thought you might want to sleep in this morning," Quincy said as he mounted the Lifecycle next to Chad.

At the conclusion of a hard minute phase, Chad caught his breath. "Woo," he breathed out. "Well, actually, I was hoping to find you here. Something I would like to discuss."

Quincy was pedaling at a strong pace, the wheel giving off a hum. "The rape scene?" he said with brow arched.

"Negative space," Chad said with a touché lift of his brow.

"You and Maylee have a history," Quincy said, more as a statement than a question.

"You don't miss much, Quincy," Chad said. He spotted a middle-aged woman wearing a tank top and gym shorts enter the room. She walked over to a floor pad in front of a mirror, where she began stretching.

"Hitchcock stated," Quincy said as he leaned forward, pedaling as though he were being chased by the police, "that to make a great film, you need three things." He lowered his pace, exhaled, and looked at Chad, his expression that of one about to reveal secret information. "You need the script, the script, and the script."

Chad's attention was momentarily diverted by the woman doing pull-downs on the Universal. She was wiry and strong-looking with rock-hard biceps. "Hitchcock also said that it's the actor's eyes that tell the story. And Angie can tell more with her eyes than any violent rape scene."

"She is a helluva of a little actress," Quincy said as his eyes followed the woman, who was now moving over to the rowing station, her back delineated by sinewy muscle.

"How about this," Chad said. "Maylee and I work with Macy today and show you this evening when you return from location shoots what we come up with." He made a *what do you think?* face at the young director. "If you don't like it, we will stick with what is in the script."

The woman approached the empty Lifecycle next to Chad and did a double take as though she had just recognized him.

"Welcome to stardom," Quincy said as an aside.

The woman said to Chad, "You were great in *Sundown at El Diablo.*"

"Thank you," Chad said. "I appreciate it."

The woman set her timer and speed on the dashboard and looked at Chad and Quincy, taking them both in with an expression that transmitted a certain hospitable warmth. "It wasn't just your dialogue," she said to Chad, "but also those silent pauses when your eyes spoke volumes."

Chad nodded a thank-you and turned to Quincy, his eyes speaking volumes.

CHAPTER 19

A FTER A SHOWER, CHAD CALLED Maylee, who was just awaking, and told her about the meeting with Quincy.

"I am meeting Angie for breakfast at the restaurant," Maylee said. "Join us."

At eight, Chad found the two women sitting in a booth at the inn restaurant. He slid in next to Maylee and said good morning to the table.

"Angie was just telling me that this is the first time she has seen you off the set," Maylee said, looking up as a waitress approached the table.

Menus were handed out and drink orders were placed.

"Nothing personal, Angie," Chad said, "but to give my best performance as Edgar Smith, I needed to keep a distance, not just from you but also from all the other actors."

"I thought that might be it," Angie said as she offered an agreeable smile, crinkling the corners of her eyes, giving her the look of someone older.

Chad had noticed her ability to transform, not her appearance exactly, but more the persona she was presenting.

"Did you know, Chad," Maylee said, "that Angie also grew up in a trailer park in Barstow?"

Chad said to Angie, "Really?"

"Macy and I have a lot in common," Angie said.

"Desert girls," Chad said, as the waitress returned with two coffees and a tea.

"I told Angie the crux of your conversation with Quincy," Maylee said under her breath to Chad. The waitress stood over the table, notepad in hand.

After they placed their orders, Chad said to Angie, "Maylee and I both feel that the rape scene should be eliminated."

He took stock of Angie, who was listening intently, her eyes attentive, her posture erect but not overly so.

"But," Chad continued, "the scene should show Edgar grabbing hold of Macy and throwing her on the sofa—a look of shock in her eyes—before cutting to Macy alone in the trailer, revealing her feelings through facial expressions, which, by the way, you are very good at."

For the next ten minutes Chad and Maylee went over the various ways Angie could show her emotions after the rape. They discussed camera angles, facial expression, and "an aura of the power of silence," as Maylee had described it.

The crash of plates and glass hitting the floor drew their attention to a busboy who had dropped a tray full of food. Another busboy rushed over with a broom and mop and assisted with the cleanup.

"Well," Angie said, looking across the table at Chad and Maylee, "when I first read the screenplay, I noticed that unlike the book, it included the actual rape scene."

The waitress came over and said there would be a delay in bringing their food.

"That crash we heard," Chad said, opening his hands to the table, "was our food."

"Manager said your breakfast is on the house," the waitress replied.

"Fair enough," Maylee said as she smiled a thank-you. She turned her attention back to Angie.

"I am all for it," Angie said. "Let the audience imagine, through Macy's silence, the horror of the moment."

In Chad's room, the three discussed the scene. Then the two actors rehearsed, with Maylee offering pointers.

Playing Edgar Smith away from the set threw Chad off his actor's rhythm, but the main focus was on Macy after the rape.

By late afternoon, they had the scene down. They decided to wait in the lobby for Quincy, and then perform for him.

As they approached the hotel lobby, Quincy entered through the sliding glass doors, which swooshed open. He wore an expression of disgruntled fatigue as though he had encountered problems on the shoot.

"Quincy," Chad said as he, Maylee, and Angie approached the director, "might we have a word?"

Quincy, startled, twitched—his shoulders flinching, his head bolting up—before composing himself. "Do I have a choice?" He motioned toward a sitting area off the lobby.

Maylee and Chad sat across a coffee table from the young director and younger actress. Chad said, "We have spent all day discussing, rehearsing, and tweaking the rape scene."

Quincy grimaced at Chad as though he were an annoying insect. "Stick to acting, Chad." He stood as though preparing to leave.

"Quincy," Maylee said with real anger. "Sit." She flashed a look at him and said softly, "Please. Hear us out."

Quincy exhaled and folded himself back in his chair. "I'm listening."

Maylee splayed her fingers out in front of herself. "Come to the conference room and let us show you what we have come up with." She bunched up her shoulders and lifted her hands as if surrendering.

Quincy sat there, his lips pursed tight, his eyes two angry slits.

"May I say something?" Angie asked.

Quincy grimaced: *Yes.*

"I understand Macy; I lived her life." Her compelling eyes, gleaming with intuitive power, captured Quincy's attention. "Ten minutes?" She lifted her brow, her gaze still on Quincy.

Quincy threw his hands out in front of himself and stood. "All right, let's get to it."

In the conference room, Chad explained to Quincy, "We thought that right after Edgar rips off Macy's blouse, we should cut to the aftermath."

Quincy said nothing, his arms folded across his chest, waiting.

After Chad and Angie did the scene leading up to the rape, Chad turned off the overhead lights, leaving only a table lamp to provide dim lighting, which cast a somber mood. "Angie, could you do the scene lying on the table?" he said as he patted the large round table that they had sat around for the meeting on the day before production.

Angie was wearing cutoffs, a white T-shirt, and flip-flops. She slipped out of her footwear then climbed atop the table and lay in a fetal position. Maylee had gotten a blanket from her room, which she now used to cover up the young actress.

"I'm going to need a minute," Angie said. She took a breath; her eyes took on a faraway hollow look and her lips pooched as a stillness settled over her.

Shortly after this, a low guttural moan came out of Angie's mouth, her expression contorted in pain. But it was her eyes that revealed a wounded hurt; they were welling with tears, which began streaming down her cheeks.

The moan grew to a crescendo until stopping abruptly. Angie brought her legs up to her chest, her arms secured tight around her knees. She began to whimper, her expression closing in. Her eyes, now puffy, fluttered shut as her lower lip trembled, her face a ghostly white.

"Cut," Quincy said. "That was remarkable."

Angie sat up, her feet dangling over the edge, as the color returned to her face and her eyes regained their vibrancy.

The room fell quiet. Chad glanced at Maylee, whose arms were crossed over her chest as though protecting herself. The corners of her eyes were in a downward slant, and her mouth was pooched open.

"Well," Chad said to Quincy.

"I still—"

"Tell you what," Chad cut in. "Let's film the rape scene with the body double and then all of us watch the dailies with and without the rape scene. Then we'll see which tells a better story."

CHAPTER 20

C HAD AWOKE EARLY THE NEXT morning and went out on the patio. He had gotten used to the sight of the darkened desert, the bold shadows of sand. Today was his last day of filming, and his mind was on overload. He had to get back into character, the long day off yesterday, away from the set, having taken him out of his acting rhythm.

He needed to concentrate on today's shoot and nothing else. He decided to go to the fitness room and get in a good workout on the Universal and the Lifecycle.

The fitness room was dark. Chad hit the switch next to the door and headed over to the Universal. He decided to start with the pull-down bar, setting the weight at seventy pounds. He began the repetitive motion of pulling the bar down to his chest and back up again—down, up, down, up, his mind and body settling into the routine.

After thirty minutes of strenuous resistance training, he moved on to the Lifecycle. He was getting himself back into Edgar mode—that mean, cantankerous, odious man.

Chad's concentration was broken by the sound of the door opening. It was the fit woman in the tank top from the other day.

"Good morning," she said.

"Morning," Chad said in a neutral voice.

The woman seemed to get the hint and went to the Universal, where she began her workout.

Chad began increasing his speed, past one hundred rotations per minute, as he envisioned Edgar ripping off Macy's blouse and tossing her to the floor. Then he envisioned the body double taking over, as Edgar tugged violently at her jeans that had been doctored to rip easily.

He saw in his mind his body atop that of the struggling woman as he reached down and opened his zipper, all while the struggle continued.

Then would come the close-up of his sweaty face, his eyes wild and evil-looking, and lastly the climax, when both bodies relaxed and he rolled himself off. It would be his last scene, this acting gig over and done with.

He thought of Maylee's most recent poem:

> A shift in the paradigm
> From when last they met
> As they advance wittingly
> In pursuit of their dreams
> To live the life imagine,
> Having met with success
> Unexpected in common hours,
> Fate intervenes as a
> New beginning arrives,
> In the land of movie-making dreams.

She had poached from Thoreau, but the great writer's words were very right for Chad and Maylee. They *were* both in pursuit of their dreams to live the life imagined.

Beads of perspiration trickling down Chad's cheek snapped him from his reverie. He checked the dashboard and slowed to a steady pace. The woman came over to the bike next to him. Chad got off, wiped his face with a towel, and said, "Have a good day."

"If all goes well," Quincy told Chad as he came on the set, "we can watch the dailies back at the inn this evening."

The morning shoot was delayed because of a snag with one of the cameras, and Chad was worried that things might go awry, but finally it was all good.

Quincy said, "Action!"

It took four long, difficult hours, but at last the filming was done, just as Chad had imagined in the fitness room earlier.

With his work on this movie complete, the first thing Chad did was to go back to his room and shave off that hideous facial hair. He studied his clean-shaven self. "Hello, stranger. Good to see you again."

Later that evening, after dinner, which Chad enjoyed with Maylee and Angie, the three met Quincy at a room set up specifically for screening.

It was like entering a small movie theater, with big cushy chairs arranged in front of a large screen. A projector was atop a table at the rear of the space.

"Okay," Quincy said, "please have a seat. I have cut it so that we first see it with the rape scene. The second cut is without it."

Quincy started the projector, turned off the lights, and sat.

The rape scene with the body double was violently horrifying, a signature part of Quincy's filmmaker repertoire. Chad could hardly believe that it was he playing this crazed white trash character. He was so damn convincing—horrifyingly so.

The second had the violence of Edgar attacking Macy, before cutting to Macy curled up in anguishing distress. By taking out the actual rape, the aftermath became more riveting in terms of Macy's pain, leaving much to the viewer's imagination.

Quincy flicked on the lights and stood in front of the screen. He shook his head as he grinned a begrudging grin. "A great director said, 'Filmmaking can be a democratic process.'"

As if on cue, Chad, Maylee, and Angie leaned forward in their chairs.

"So, as much as I hate deleting that beautifully violent rape," Quincy said, throwing his hands out to his side, "we will do it"—he brought his hands up in front of his chest, his palms up—"your way."

Again, as if on cue, the three let out a gratifying cheer.

Chad asked, "Who was that great director?"

Quincy laughed a self-deprecating laugh. "Me. I just made it up."

Angie asked Quincy if she could go over a few things for tomorrow's shoot.

Chad and Maylee excused themselves.

Out in the hallway, Chad said to Maylee, "I bought a bottle of cabernet. Join me for a drink on my patio?"

A half-moon eased its way up into the moody-blue night sky, the hills partially illuminated, the desert once again in shadows. Chad and Maylee, with drinks in hand, sat on his patio taking in the muted darkness and each other's company, with a mutual understanding of the shift in the paradigm.

Chad thought of a line from "The Sound of Silence" by Simon and Garfunkel: "people talking without speaking, people hearing without listening."

"Seeing you on the set as Edgar Smith was hard," Maylee said with a wince.

"I could tell," Chad said. "I needed to be that way to give the best performance."

"You did that." Maylee reached over and stroked his freshly shaved chin. "I see you no longer are *that* way."

"A toast," Chad said as he raised his glass, which Maylee clinked with hers with, "to living the life we have imagined."

"And," Maylee said, her gaze on a stratum of clouds that were glowing in sections as they passed by the moon, "let us not forget, unexpected in common hours."

"Your poem is coming to fruition," Chad said.

"We must give a nod to Mr. Thoreau," Maylee said as she reached for Chad's hand, her fingers interlacing his.

Chad brought her hand over his chest. "Does that life imagined have you and me together?"

"In my dreams it does," Maylee said, her eyes asking, *And in your dreams?*

Chad came over in front of Maylee and got down on his knee. "Will you marry me?"

"One condition." Maylee lifted a finger and said, "Make that two."

"Anything."

"One," Maylee said leaning forward, her hand on Chad's cheek. "Small ceremony, just Monty and Cara." She looked at Chad for his reaction.

"And?"

"Our honeymoon is a road trip with the best man and bridesmaid."

"Now," Chad said as he kissed Maylee on the cheek and leaned back, "that is what I call LA easy."

ABOUT THE AUTHOR

Much like Chad Carson, I quit my government job and moved to Oakwood Apartments, for singles, in Sherman Oaks. I worked odd jobs from a day labor center, took acting classes, and hired a photographer to help me create an actor's portfolio. Eventually, I got work as an extra in films, but I had no luck obtaining the elusive Screen Actors Guild card. I came close once to getting the lead in a low-budget film and was even told I had won the part, but then it vanished—nothing LA easy about that one.

After a year, dispirited and broke, I returned home to Bethesda, Maryland. My first month home, I signed on with Central Casting in Washington, DC, and was picked for a local commercial advertising a ski mask that was invented by a dentist, who saw my portfolio and insisted on me—he liked my smile. And voilà, I had my SAG card. But any thoughts of leaving for LA were a no-go since I had met my future wife, Tina. The rest, as they say, is history.

LA Easy is my version of what possibly might have happened if I had returned to the West Coast and pursued a career in film. The word *if* is, for me, the basis of fiction writing, or in my case conjuring up another possible life. But in the end, much must be left unknown, with only our imaginations to provide what might have been.

The young man in the portfolio photos seems like a person from another life, a dreamworld. And it is a failed dream as far as success in film goes, but it taught me a life lesson that no school could have ever provided.

Dennis
McKay

Height: 6' 2" / Weight: 195 lbs.
Hair: Light Brown / Eyes: Blue

Printed in the United States
by Baker & Taylor Publisher Services